Chronicles of Sexual Escapades –
The George Manfield Biography

# Pablo

# Chronicles of Sexual Escapades – The George Manfield Biography

Olympia Publishers
*London*

www.olympiapublishers.com
OLYMPIA PAPERBACK EDITION

Copyright © Pablo 2023

The right of Pablo to be identified as author of
this work has been asserted in accordance with sections 77 and 78 of
the Copyright, Designs and Patents Act 1988.

All Rights Reserved

No reproduction, copy or transmission of this publication
may be made without written permission.
No paragraph of this publication may be reproduced,
copied or transmitted save with the written permission of the publisher,
or in accordance with the provisions
of the Copyright Act 1956 (as amended).

Any person who commits any unauthorised act in relation to
this publication may be liable to criminal
prosecution and civil claims for damage.

A CIP catalogue record for this title is
available from the British Library.

ISBN: 978-1-80439-037-5

This is a work of fiction.
Names, characters, places and incidents originate from the writer's
imagination. Any resemblance to actual persons, living or dead, is
purely coincidental.

First Published in 2023

Olympia Publishers
Tallis House
2 Tallis Street
London
EC4Y 0AB

Printed in Great Britain

# Dedication

Dedicated to GM.

# Acknowledgements

Thanks to George Manfield.

# Chapter One

# The Visit

I write, putting myself into the shoes of a young African-British man, as he tells me the world-wide, wild adventures of his sexual escapades. Passive presentations make the reportage too impersonal and I hope my chosen style drives home the intended result. Moreover, all names used are pseudonyms for legal reason and to prevent the chain of lawsuits that may likely follow. All names and companies and places of interest used have been changed for legal reasons. Although some are the right mentions, others are but a work of fiction. You may read this account either as total fiction or as a true story, whichever way you want, but that will not put the author in jeopardy and at the same time protect the narrator and his subjects. It will not also change the storyline narrated but from what I gathered, most people may in a way identify with it either now or in the future.

    A tale of shocking revelations shrouded and well-protected in secrecy. This is a closed network of like-minded people in their own world and will ward off any intruder seen as a betrayal or potential betrayal. The discoveries are like unveiling the infamous mafia cartel. He only tells me he was making known those revelations to understand what it is like to be in his world while he may discover great ideas which could lead to his recovery. The activities so described were even too graphically depicted and explicit that I wondered if any publisher would accept the manuscript; hence, the lighter note I took. The entire story sounded untrue to me until he proved me wrong with pictures, chats online and followed up calls right in front of me. I cannot publish the documentary evidence due to the agreement reached with George Manfield. Famous pictures and artistes, Facebook accounts, uncountable and different online chats, traditional cell phone calls and text messaging were made available but well-kept and coded to avoid leakage. The gentleman – very unassuming and with well-coiffed hair and elegantly dressed to kill – sat before me as he relaxed to pour out his heart. He was of tall height, had well cared for chocolate-coloured skin and athletically built of a sort. He looked well-manicured and attracted attention. At a moment, he would boastfully brag about what he did and at other, he would regretfully opine. I was torn between a happy going chap who loved what he did but regrettably wished to come out. I couldn't read his mind, but all I deduced was a guy who needed help. He had approached me because he felt my speech during a seminar which he attended had touched on salient issues he was battling with. He was hopeful I was going to be able to offer some direction of help. All these while I tried to find a point in time to prove what he told me were lies but couldn't find any. This is a guy who by all standards came across as a very masculine and well-mannered with high doses of testosterone boiling up in him. In addition to that, he sounded very religious and even gave me phrases of religious quotations during our discourse.

He was neatly dressed and I could see he loved fashion. His coat was impeccably pressed with a spotted nice cotton shirt. He matched up with nice accessories, and I noticed his expensive Rolex watch that he wore. The reason for our meeting was hinged on counselling terms. Surprisingly, he came with a small notebook and a pen which he told me was to jot down the wisdom he would receive. That put me in a very uncomfortable position as at this time I knew what I said to this guy mattered most. I had delivered a speech recently during a summit and gave my cell number out to the audience to contact me if they needed help or for further counselling. I least expected to receive a call from this thirty-five-years-old with a master's degree in law, saddled with enormous problems which could easily unmake him and cause great disgrace at least within the geographical area he found himself. He was working as a consultant to one of the mining firms in his location.

I have tried to chronicle his experiences and adventures as he presented it, being particular about the rawness and vulgar presentations which I have penned down euphemistically. I am sure without censorship of the choice of words he uttered, the entire piece would have been seen as another porn story. I ask for your pardon if I wrongfully use a word that may not bring the allusion he wanted and intended. I know many people have experiences of such and may disagree with some of my choices of words but it is because I try to appeal to a wider spectrum of audience and with great decorum and civility being adhered to. This is without recourse to your individual rights and general human rights enshrined in the many documents whether in your country or outside your country.

Before we set out to talk, he had pleaded anonymity since he did not want to be known but confided in me that he really needed help to stop his sexual escapades. He presented himself as George Manfield.

I have tried to summarise his story but careful to capture the entire story told.

He had narrated his life with emphasis on his sexual adventures, experiences and escapades which he vividly explained.

Don't mistake this story as told to be from an unmarried man. He was married at the time of narrating it. He had done stuff when unmarried but still more stuff when he got married. The issues of sex had nothing to do with married or unmarried people from my counselling experience in all these years.

I have maintained that marriage was not a panacea to sexual immorality and promiscuity. Any amorous escapades need to be dealt with before venturing into a well-meaningful love and sexual relationship to last. And that getting married was also not an antidote to shying away from same-sex adventures or womanising. All these need to be rooted from source. They always come back to haunt the victim if not dealt with psychologically, physiologically, emotionally, academically, sociologically, physically and spiritually.

In the event of getting holistic help, it also behoves on the person in question to embrace with the certainty and desire to and for change. The danger is solving one aspect and leaving the others unchecked. The remaining unsolved aspect often times can spoil the successes chalked in the other areas because one bad nut causes damage to the whole lot.

# Chapter Two

## Early Upbringing

I sat around a table of guys on an outing rendezvous. I have always loved outing even at an early age with my parents. Based on my early chat with George Manfield, I tried testing the waters to know what they think, their likes and their sexual activities.

I had good response for their likes and thoughts but a complete shut off when it had to do with sexual escapades. It wasn't surprising to me because as a counsellor, I know the topic was even a taboo to discuss in some religious and societal settings, in some homes and hardly discussed among friends. It seems no one wants to be found out what he or she does in the closet when no one is watching. People find the topic a no-go area but thanks to recent talks, seminars, sex education, that jinx is broken but still people are yet to come to terms with accepting it as an everyday life issue that shouldn't be left to only the married or religious leaders. I wasn't going to receive any new ideas since none of these guys wanted to talk. This was to confirm what George had told me earlier. And really so, people shied away from such topics and most especially getting to know them in that line. Again, they all told me they had girlfriends which was also something George asked me to check out.

It was quite interesting as they shielded themselves with

their girlfriends and wives. A lady once retorted that all the most eligible bachelors were gays and the most handsome men were also either married or gays. As profound as it may sound, I disagreed in part to digress in whole. I hold the view of debunking unsubstantiated and un-researched statistical findings people put out there for global consumption. Some of these sayings only come as assumptions and personal thoughts and inclinations and lack proper research. So I was so shocked with the answers so given because George had cautioned me earlier.

So, after all, people think walking and going out with a lady means they are insulated from same-sex temptations or have freed themselves as such. That to me is a total deception and a lie. There have been instances some couples have walked up to me and later found out that both were homosexuals and are in what we call arranged or planned marriages for convenience' sake. They do so to shy away from public ridicule and the incessant public homophobic outcry against same-sex partners at least in major places on the Earth's surface until recently.

The early upbringing of people can go a long way to make or unmake them. The exposure of people, the communication used, the social basket mix, the orientation, the religion, the family, the geographical location, the thoughts and aspirations of individuals and families alike and the overall acceptance or condemnation of certain acts so observed all play a vital role in the shaping and reshaping of the total man or woman.

I do not begrudge homosexuals or heterosexuals or bisexuals or pansexuals or omnisexuals or unisexuals and all the others because until you find out the early upbringing, one can hardly appreciate how far others have come.

# Chapter Three

# Born in South Africa, Bred in Ghana

I was born in South Africa, an African economic giant country with abundant natural resources coupled with a rich culture and sad history of apartheid. The apartheid had eaten to the very core of human life and fabric to the extent that, as a means of consolation, the oppressed resorted to music. This is the reason why South African songs are loved because of the emotions the singers bring forth. Some of these emotions have some roots from the apartheid era. The roots from apartheid had forced many to turn to religion as a means of leverage and gathering. My family practiced Christianity as a religion and the children were forced to attend church every Sunday. There couldn't be an excuse to exempt oneself since all the holes to explore were sealed. Attending church was not bad at all since I got to meet my friends and it gave me some time to hang out with them after closing.

With South Africa as a mining giant, my dad had to relocate to Ghana because my mum was born Ghanaian. My dad thought with his experience in South Africa as an electrical engineer, there would be room for him in Ghana as well since the country was also known for its huge mining virtually of every ore. We moved to Ghana at my tender age of seven and I vividly remembered the move and my past life in South Africa.

There wasn't any sharp contrast then as the livelihood was

about the same with the exception that Ghana was not under the apartheid system. I also thought that these apartheid emotions may have precipitated the move to settle in Ghana by my dad.

My mum had made all the preparations for our coming that helped us to quickly settle in and to acclimatise. Now we all could live under the same roof as a family of six. My mum had spoken to a friend of hers at a mine in Ghana and secured a job for Dad. This made the transition very smooth for all of us. In as much as I sometimes miss South African, Ghana became more than home for me.

So I am a born South African, bred and schooled in Ghana and London and a naturalised British. This is because of the geographical locations I got exposed to and count myself blessed for getting the best out of every place.

In Ghana, I got to know my relatives, many of them, but chiefly my uncle who was a diocesan bishop in one of the orthodox churches. Due to this, we all attended his church. I found that intriguing as it meant my dad changing from his Roman Catholic faith to become a Methodist. That was a huge sacrifice we all made even in our early years.

I remember the first time at church when we got introduced, there were rousing shouts of welcome in local dialects which I didn't understand then but do now. The church showed support for us and our immediate friends were children of my bishop uncle though they were relationally cousins. There was this cousin, Robert, I loved so much because we were of the same age and later stayed in the same classroom. Church wasn't any different though, but the Methodist sung more hymns in my opinion than the Roman Catholics. Church was lovely and so were the children as we settled in at the Sunday School Department. It was great.

I was later taken to the school owned by the mine my dad worked with. The school was a mix of white and blacks kids, unlike South African where we were segregated. My first day at school was not so comfortable because I never had been in class with a white child. More so, their tongue in terms of the speed at which they spoke made it difficult to comprehend. But this was soon to change as even at the early age, I knew I was intelligent which attracted more people to me. So schooling in Ghana was no different. I enjoyed the attention and the big ups. I made friends with almost every child in class but selected who became close buddies. There was this pretty girl of mix-race parentage that I fancied so much but really at that age never knew what it meant to love.

My school had many showers so we could shower down after our breaks or physical education lesson before entering our classrooms. In the showers, we poked fun at each other and teased ourselves. Again as small as I was, I never knew the line of thinking of some of the older boys, but I remember they used to make fun of some boys having crooked willies and others were teased of having big or small willies. I didn't find that amusing, but sooner or later I became the chief teaser because I wanted to avoid being bullied.

My school had the best of facilities I could think of and tried making comparison when I grew up with present-day facilities and realised that the facilities were best during my time in primary school.

I got involved in many school activities which I enjoyed, all without regrets. I enjoyed every moment, but at home I was known as the quiet type. I knew I wasn't quiet, but my dad's temperament when a child fooled around kept me at bay. What covered my mischief was the fact that I was the intelligent child every parent wished their children aspired to. My report from school kept me in the good books of my dad.

I had a sweet savvy for the best so I worked harder in school so my dad gave me the best rewards. I was the toast of my dad in terms of academics. I was the fun type who never fought with anyone but I realised I had my dad's bad temperament too.

I graduated from lower primary through to upper primary and soon was to choose a college to continue. I knew it was going to be outside town since there were no many schools around. I got to choose the school I wanted to go. At first, my mum wanted a mix and boarding school. I also preferred a boys' boarding school because my cousin Fred that I was in the same class with chose a boys; boarding school. What I never wanted was to attend the same school with him so while he went to Prempeh College, I went to Presbyterian Boys' Secondary School in Accra. It happened to be one of the best science schools in Ghana then and perfectly suited my science programme I had chosen.

In college, I made new friends and this time, they were all boys, except for the girls we went to chase from other schools. It was quite an experience as we all came from different backgrounds and bonded by our affiliation to our school and with different goals to work on.

At Presby Boys too, the teasing continued as some other boys got bullied in many ways. Some got their food seized. Others were beaten and few were discriminated upon. What I never understood was the fact that the teasing had always been over how someone looked like or behaved. These came with chosen nicknames imposed on people. There was no saying of I don't like the name. It is either you had yours or you were given one by your peers, juniors or seniors. It added to the fun as well. At college, every junior boy was assigned to a senior boy to serve but some seniors went the extra mile to mentor their 'sons' as we termed it. It was good having a dad in school who rescued me from other seniors who wanted to beat me. In short, he protected me.

As boys, we did everything together and were not shy of ourselves, but one experience on arrival from vacation to school would change the way I behaved.

As the school reopened and we had arrived early and as usual, people narrated their vacation experiences. Some who had done something special like traveling shared their story and others also lied to get accepted. I was quite lucky since I got to travel on almost every vacation to South Africa because I had uncles, aunties and cousins there. My dad never wanted us to lose or forget our roots.

We gathered in one cubicle as we chatted and ate as more students trickled in one after the other. But whatever the case was, one was permitted to sleep anywhere since school was not in full session and we were few as well. Upon arrival of all students, everyone went to their designated houses and cubicles.

During the chat, I had this mate who even wasn't a close pal sitting behind me but kept his distance to me close. We were also in different classes, different cubicles but in the same house. In fact, our bodies leaned in together and no one complained about it. We all laughed and talked unendingly deep into the night because there were no classes the next day until school officially opened on the following Monday. We had gone to school on Thursday because there was always the opportunity to come earlier but latest by Saturday preceding the official Monday opening, when all must report by then. We continued in our chats with stories upon stories. This time, my mate Kyle drew closer and pulled himself behind me. I could feel his penis pressing behind me, but I couldn't say it. He made fun as all laughed. I felt the uneasiness, but it seemed he found pleasure in doing so. This time, he was closer behind me. I sat a step lower than his position and really felt the compression of his penis at my back. It was late and one by one, we started scattering to our various cubicles. I went to my cubicle, found a bed in the corner of the room and slept. Later, Kyle also came to my cubicle and said he wanted to sleep beside me. This was news to me and was the first time for me to share a bed with anyone. It all started out as fun leading to more chats. He would not leave, so I realised he was serious but never thought anything happening again beyond what had transpired which only the two of us knew about. As small as these monkey-type beds were, we both managed to sleep on it. There were two more people to join me in the cubicle but got to know they had gone to town and were not coming so I had to lock the door finally.

Kyle began fondling me all over and eventually holding my penis which he played with, rubbing it up and down. This was a novel experience. As much as I felt uneasy, it was gratifying. He rubbed the shaft of my penis and when I even tried escaping his reach, he held onto it tighter. He finally let go after he had finished stroking me and told me to do same to him. I was damn afraid and didn't do it. He also tried kissing me which I refused. The night was very short as we lay in bed doing our own thing. We got up early and Kyle went to his cubicle. He later brought some breakfast which we all ate, but, seriously, I knew the action the night before was not going to repeat itself. I kept it close to my chest fearing to even tell my best friend.

These meetings went on for several times, even when school was in full session; Kyle had a place in the plantations and we went to play there all alone. I didn't know it was gayism at that time and only learned about it recently. I never knew his stroking and rubbing the shaft of my penis till I released was masturbation either. In terms of sexuality, I was very naïve. There were times we both went to bath together and Kyle would use soap to masturbate me and asked me to do same. The way our showers were, there was no way anyone could think something like that would go on but it went on. I grew an interest for this and it became the norm almost every now and then. That kept us together as friends for a long time till we graduated.

My best friend Joseph in school was oblivious to my encounters with Kyle. I kept it away from him, but he found out one time and confronted me. I couldn't deny it and told him all that had transpired. I was afraid he was going to betray me. In fact, all our meetings had revolved around masturbation and kissing which I did not find amusing at all. Joseph was the shy type and hardly joined in conversations; he was the direct opposite of me. Mysteriously, I don't know how it happened, I found myself and Joseph getting into this as well. I have tried to recollect where it all started between us but have found no clues yet. For Joseph, it was me masturbating him all the time. He seemed to enjoy it too. There were few times he also performed it on me. Then we graduated into kissing each other. By this time, I seemed to have had gotten so much into kissing and masturbation. There was one senior who I got involved with too. He was one of the school football stars.

At some point, I wanted to know if this was what had been going on all this time on campus. I had heard of homosexuals, but I couldn't believe it was happening to me. Moreover, I also couldn't ask if some other boys were into that and whether he knew anyone. It was a tight-lip affair where no one talked much and no one made enquiries in order to keep identities secret or unknown.

There were times Joseph and I would skip evening prep hours to engage in our new-found activity. Times that I went to study, I went with Kyle. There were times we sat around a big table and played with our legs underneath to no one would notice. We had practiced this so well so that we could fondle each other with our legs under the table. It became a normal and regular routine for us; a ritual we only practiced with no one knowing. We faked studying but in our own way made love under the table. This behaviour became a feature for me with Kyle and Joseph not knowing anything existed. I did not want to believe I was gay, which I am not, but developed affection for the same sex. My understanding of a gay guy was someone who was attracted to only same sex. For me, that wasn't the case and felt some relief because it was unheard of in those times to say or be found out.

Even till today in Ghana, it is illegal to indulge in a same-sex affair. South Africa legalised it sometime later.

My sexual encounters and fun with Kyle and my friend notwithstanding, I had a girlfriend from another girls school around and visited during our free exeats. If it were today, I would have been branded a player or Casanova. I was appropriate when it came to sex with women and men. So there was never a time I felt I wanted to have sex that I had been deprived. If I didn't get to sleep with my guys, the women were there and vice versa. All these sexual affairs did not happen until I entered university. This time, I really did not know who I had become and what I wanted sexually.

George emphatically told me that he would pass for a virgin, since he had not had sex with anyone and that his sex life actually began after he got into bed with Edward, a senior from Presby Boys Secondary School at the university.

We vacationed and went home and became more curious to know what people were up to. At the same time, I was afraid to tell anyone but continued masturbating. I visited my cousin Robert one weekend and played some video games together. I slept over at his place. I wanted to share my experience with him but this is a cousin whose dad was a bishop. Things didn't click and I thought I would keep it to myself. I couldn't so we went to bed and happened to share bed with him. That evening, as we lay down, so many thoughts came to mind and I was picturing Kyle and myself. Robert got to know I was hard and started teasing me. He later was also hard and as the night would have it, jokingly we masturbated. But for him, we did it to ourselves without touching each other. A knock came at the door in the process so we hurriedly pulled up our pants and pretended nothing had happened. My little cousin entered and slept right in between us, saying he was afraid. This was the first and was to be the last Robert and I did that. I perceived that had it not been for my little cousin, we might have explored ourselves. And this was happening right in the mission house; the irony of it.

My relationships between Kyle and Joseph continued till we completed college and left campus and that was the last time we ever did anything like that. The relationship with my senior was a one off-fling in school back then.

We all graduated and found our own paths in life.

# Chapter Four

# Masturbation

Having engaged in all these habits, I developed the passion of masturbating alone and did that just anywhere and when the slightest opportunity presented itself. Since this time I was going to stay at home for some time before our results came, and being left alone at home most of the time, I always masturbated. I used and tried all kinds of stuff. Finding a bottle and oiling it and using it. I masturbated using Vaseline, shea butter, soap and at times nothing at all. I became so much addicted to it that my penis got bruised as I was over doing it. Once it got bruised, then I would wait for it to heal first. When I was alone, I masturbated just everywhere and anywhere in the house. I never got involved with people from my community or neighbourhood because I was afraid they might expose me. This continued and of all my life, the period after secondary school till I entered university was the time I masturbated the most. I became addicted and masturbated every day and in some instances, two or even three times a day. My favourite place was to pretend to go and have a bath and did my own thing in the shower. I masturbated looking at myself in the mirror and how I twisted my waist and jerked off. It was fun and gratifying. I realised from the mirror image that I was well-endowed and pride myself with it.

There were times I masturbated watching porn to see and

know the styles and skills they practiced. I also liked masturbating when I could see people outside, but they couldn't see me. It gave me some joy. It more or less became a fetish I enjoyed. I will not say I hated masturbation or loved it, but it kept my involvement with other guys at bay. So I became a lone ranger for security's sake and for fear of being found out which I knew would be disgraceful. So my masturbation went on.

There were times I even got involved later in life with sons of pastors when we jerked off. I did that with many people from different spheres of life.

# Chapter Five

## First Degree

I got to attend University of Ghana. At the university, I met my senior from Presby Boys whom I had a short fling with. Somehow, I was happy. What I realised too was that at the university, no one cared or monitored anyone. I met him for the first time at the university and went to see his hall of residence. He was at Legon Hall Annex A. They were three people accommodated in the room. I was at Commonwealth Hall. As a first-year student, I kept my mind off everything to concentrate on my studies. Once in a while, I went out and at times visited my senior, Edward.

I was in my room one night when Edward came around. We spoke for a while and he told me we should go to his place. Since it was the same campus, it was not a big problem. None of his roommates were around when we got in. I got to know they had both gone home for the weekend. So that night, we were all alone by ourselves and had the whole room to ourselves.

This was going to be a proper sexual adventure as Edward brought some petroleum gel / Vaseline and condoms out. We turned off the lights and started caressing each other endlessly. We kissed and Edward sucked my nipples. The sensation was heavenly without being rude to any religion. After a long haul of touching, he took the Vaseline and smeared it all over my penis and I realised it gave a smooth movement as he begun masturbating me. I did the same to him. He gave me a condom and I must confess it was news since it hadn't happened before, not even with a woman. He took the condom, opened it and rolled it over my penis. He smeared some Vaseline 'round the rubber and held my penis to his ass and directed my penetration. I wondered how my penis would fit into this small ass but he told me to try slipping it in gently, which I managed to do. He moaned at first but once I entered, he told me to take my time and gently thrust in and out. I continued as he groaned with satisfaction till I ejaculated. He removed the condom and started stroking me with his left hand as his masturbated himself with the right hand. He released some cum and we cleaned the mess with a towel he gave me. The whole experience was new but fun though.

We went to sleep closely hugging each other. I must say we couldn't sleep well as once in a while though we wanted to sleep, he would be rubbing his ass on my penis and vice versa. I remember just around the early hours of about four in the morning, Edward slipped down and the next thing was my penis in his mouth. He sucked me over and over till I came in his mouth which he spilled away into the towel we had used to clean up earlier. He told me it was called a blowjob and that I should try it. I refused to do it and never did. It was just disgusting to me. Moreover, it never felt right for me. For Edward, he introduced me to anal sex and blowjob. Others had only been caressing and masturbating till then.

I went on with my academics but meetings with Edward went on from time to time at different places. At times, we would have sex on the rooftop of his hall of residence. At times, too, in the stairways of some lecture rooms at night where the place was quiet and isolated. There was always a new place to have fun with such a big campus like ours.

All these notwithstanding, I also dedicated time to excel in my course work. Near our school was the University of Professional Studies just a stone-throw away. I and some friends had gone there and I met a guy called O'Neil. We had gone to see a girlfriend of one of my friends. I personally had a girlfriend at Volta Hall on campus and did our own thing.

The night after I had sex with Edward, I visited Genevieve and convinced her to have sex and we did. With her, I had sex almost every week while I still kept my homosexual fantasies going on. There were times it became difficult to please so I would pretend to be sick and used it as an excuse. This went on for some time. I had other ladies coming my way. Some I had sex with several times in their rooms and others in rented guest houses, depending on whether I had money.

Edward was a chain smoker and he indulged in marijuana too. He told me that when he was smoking and I had sex with him, he did not feel any pain. I also started smoking as well, but mine was on and off. After all, I was the keeper of marijuana for some friends but never smoked. Trying it wasn't hard for me since I had always hung out among some smokers.

# Chapter Six

# O'Neil

In all these relationship, I never committed myself until I met O'Neil also on campus. He was from a very good home and stayed with both parents like myself, but the only difference was I stayed with my step mum after my mum died. He was a nice guy and a course mate. We had been in school but never met until the third year when we did managerial economics as a course together. He was affable and kind. He seemed to like me so much that he never wanted to separate himself from me. For him, it was to be a good friendship at first. There were times I went with him to his house, we would sleep and return the next day. His mum was very friendly and welcoming. He started catering for me as in buying me groceries and bringing me home-cooked food anytime he went home.

This went on for some time until one day in his house, he couldn't restrain himself and kissed me. This sparked the whole engine and opened a new chapter. In all my relationships, O'Neil was the one person despite the attraction we had for each other that I really liked as a brother. His mum actually treated us as such. He was older though.

Most of our sexual encounters happened in his house. For him, I was the best friend and lover. This was my first unofficial relationship. Even after school, we would still be together. With O'Neil, the room, the bath house and at times in their sitting hall when no one was at home were our favourite sex places. We went to great lengths in many ways. There were times I would penetrate him and had fun even on Saturdays and the next morning, we would be off to church. I knew we were not serious Christians. We grew closer and we did everything together. We shared clothes and even boxers. All was fine and there were times jealousy crept in when he saw me with other guys or ladies. Hitherto, we had managed just fine. Complaints upon complaints started to occur and finally we got separated because we happened to be chasing the same lady but we both didn't realise. For O'Neil, he wasn't too much bent on us parting, but this lady concocted stories to alienate me, I should say. In the end, neither of us got to date her because we came to know the truth but then an ugly argument reared its head between O'Neil and I. I was with him for some time. We were friends for a long time before we got into each other and then separated. We are not enemies but not as we used to be either. From school and still counting, we could be clocking about a decade plus of friendship had it not been the little scuffle that ensued then.

For all my relationships, O'Neil was special to me and I hold a place in my heart for him even till today. He was a brother from another mother. I could have a real talk just about everything and anything with him. We shared our joys and sorrows. He was the understanding type and we went on well even if nothing sensual happened. This was a guy I could chat up for hours. We took walks together. We ate together. We virtually did everything together. It was a moment I really had a friend and a brother. I loved him to bits as he did too.

One thing O'Neil never knew was the fact that a friend of his had proposed to be with me, but I had refused. The friend kept showering me with gifts of all kinds without his knowledge, but we never did anything together. Having O'Neil was everything to me and never in my weakest moment thought of cheating. Cheating was something I hated and once I was in a relationship, be it with a man or woman, my loyalty was unquestionable.

We completed our first degree and as a valedictorian, got scholarships to study abroad. I researched many countries and with my new sex life, I looked for a freer state where I wouldn't have to be too conscious. For all these relationships I got into, they were always hidden because once I got caught, it would spell doom for me. I finally settled on London Imperial College for my masters. So London, there I went.

**The Conflict, Confusion and Bitterness**

In all my relationships, I tried to avoid conflicts from confusion that led to bitterness. But it was not to be as a great confusion soon arose, creating some bitter conflict between O'Neil and I.

The conflict had arisen from a decision he was about to make; that was to get into a normal relationship, if I must say, with a lady he found to be of marriage material. It is amazing how jealousy set in. I vehemently opposed the relationship. I had fought it to the extent that the lady in question, sensing what was ongoing between us, then decided to let the cat out of the bag. So brutal she was with the truth that she sugar-coated, spiced and made it appear all true. But frankly, a lot of the information she communicated to O'Neil was wrong.

It was at this point that I realised the relationship with emotions and a good investment was painful to lose. I had invested into it with all my resources because that was what I believed in.

Relationship with the same sex or opposite sex stood at par and had not many differences apart from the factor of a woman in the latter. It comes with the loyalty, commitment, trust, kissing, likeness, sex, communication, unity in doing things together etc. In short, it hurts to lose any partner or person in any relationship. In fact, this confusion the lady created resulted in the bitterest acrimony between O'Neil and me. We were good but I did not know O'Neil harboured great resentment and bitterness. This was to be fifteen years' worth of bitterness. I wanted him only to myself, but he felt I was too controlling.

This incident led to wars of words both oral and written. Some of the despicable things could happen were threatening of murder, pronouncement of uselessness among many. It was such a battle to win O'Neil, back but it was not to be. I got many friends of us into the picture to salvage our relationship. What was unknowing to our friends was the gay relationship. This we both couldn't tell anyone either and really seeped into our pores like cancer. Maybe, a full explanation to them would have helped but how dare any one of us, O'Neil or myself, to say it. So the war continued fiercely, emotionally, psychologically, mentally beyond psychology and physically. Only the two of us knew what exactly it was that we fought but superficially, we presented the reason as divergent views in some decision-making. Of course, it was a decision-making problem. I fought as hard as I could, but left the shores of the country in the middle of it. This time, a friend of O'Neil who was pretending to solve the issue wanted to get involved with me. He was gay and we both did not know. He better understood the situation, but again he kept mute. It was an abomination to talk about gay relationships. The bitterness raged on. I travelled. O'Neil found work and we all moved on but internally between us, but we knew we had an unfinished business. Several years apart, we finally met but still it was not to be.

I remember O'Neil might have found solace in God and advocated we stopped such a relationship since it was against our Christian principles. I loved him so fought him, but we had to let go of the relationship. That was painful and a wasted time. It was because despite gayism was illegal in our country, we had planned to let it work between us under the sheets while we present to the world that we were just the best of brothers. The deception and lies couldn't hold, so we finally had to let it go. It is surprising no one knows what actually happened up to today that made us such bitter rivals. Only we know.

After fifteen years, I decided to visit O'Neil unexpectedly. But I wasn't going to revive our relationship, only to seek forgiveness for my bad deeds. I had realised I had been very emotional while dealing with the issue that had arisen, neglecting and employing other faculties to solve the problem. No wonder I never was able to solve it.

I approached his mum who was excited to see me back, exclaiming I was a prodigal son. Of course I had been because she took me as her son from the onset and really helped us. Finally, after waiting several hours, O'Neil came, sat down, exchanged the usual pleasantries and asked me my mission. This time, I had to swallow my pride and just say sorry. He sat through the discourse and also gave his thoughts. Finally, he openly said he had forgiven me and now his spirit was free. It was the best thing to happen to me. And I think being forgiven is the best thing that can happen to any soul under the sun. Being offended comes with a lot of emotions and baggage.

Likewise, being the offender also comes with soul searching and provoking thoughts with a million unanswered questions.

We finally buried the hatchet and peace prevailed, but there was no way we could be the friends we used to be. I would have wished for that though.

I came to conclude that a relationship, be it male-to-male or female-to-female or male-to-female, were all the same.

The striking difference under the legally accepted norms of any relationship was with the latter resulting in child-bearing and former not. But in all, the principles and virtues of loyalty, trust, faithfulness, truthfulness, commitment, liking, love, sustaining the relationship, consistency and many more all hold truth in the same manner.

I never will hold one in high esteem than the other though society may disagree of one, but that doesn't make the unaccepted less sacred in terms of principles and virtues to be upheld.

**The Deceptions and Betrayals**

There are a lot that goes on in relationship but chiefly has to do with deceptions. Another incident that happened with another gay friend had to do with deceptions and betrayals. I had chatted online with a friend and we finally agreed to meet in his house. On my way to his house, I had a clean mind just for visit, but once there I saw all this preparation to have an encounter by my friend. Upon arrival, I decided to sit outside to avoid the two of us being alone in the room which could trigger any sexual encounter. The friend was pushy and insisted to come to the room even though his dad was around. He had assured me of locking the door after us and would be okay and there was no need to worry. But I resisted with all my strength and stayed outside. I was served with some fruit cocktail. We stayed chatting unendingly.

In the course of my visit, two of my host's friends came along to visit or were just passing through his place to say hello. I realised all three of them, through their conversation, liked me and took my number. Our friendship was as usual, but it was going to be a nightmare in the months to come.

I never liked my host for reasons known only to me. His friends were okay but I never liked them either. But what happened was one of his friends by name Mills showed more interest but had refused to call to chat. I got to know because my host had told me. I took his number to call him and for the first time, we chatted for a three good hours. I got to know the chemistry that existed so we continued calling and to familiarise ourselves with each other. Because we both were not living alone, most of our meet ups were at Mills' friends' houses or in hotels.

Some friends were in the navy and police forces. We had good meet ups. The bonding was great that we just loved to be close to each other all the time. Mills was secretive just as myself and kept our relationship hush hush. I lied a few times about my personality to Mills because I wasn't sure of me not being exposed but he was forthright, though I later found some traces of lies.

I went to great lengths with Mills. We both were tops but I realised later he was versatile. We just made love at the last meet up. He was so much into me and likewise. Mills had a very long penis and it was not thick. There were times he wanted to penetrate me. I fought with that until I allowed him some day. It wasn't a good feeling. It was quite painful. I never saw or felt any satisfaction with it. But that notwithstanding, we continued our sexual escapades. We rimmed each other. We sucked each other. We masturbated each other. We fucked each other. We kissed. We did all that there was to try. But we still kept our friendship in wraps.

The problem that arose was that Mills was a sex maniac. He loved sex seriously and I couldn't keep up in terms of him penetrating me but I fucked him always.

This led to my suspicions of him cheating. It was an uneasy feeling to think of Mills cheating behind my back. I read his mails and text messages to ascertain the truth. Every message alluded to the cheating, but he would argue he only chatted for fun. On numerous occasions, I felt and actually concluded but he never accepted. I gave him the benefit of doubt since I had not caught him or did not have any proof except for my instincts.

I kept blaming and accusing him of cheating which he fought back. It at times ended things in temporal separation but found ways to iron out our differences. I helped Mills financially so much so that there were times I felt being used or Mills being a gold digger. But the bottom line was I wanted him to be happy, but he was not the tameable one. He had a free spirit to explore at times dangerously. I must say we had fun and spent good times together. We got to know each other's family and I was readily accepted and that made it easier as I could now visit him at home and he could also visit me.

There were times my cousin would sleep with us in a room, but we managed to have sex. Other times, his bother would sleep with us in his room but we had sex anyway. No one suspected us and made it easy to manoeuvre without suspicions. There were times we got close to being caught but we sailed through.

It was during one of my complaints sessions that Mills really came out and told me he had cheated on me and did not deserve me. He pleaded I forgive him but wanted us to break up so I could find a better person. There was genuineness in his eyes, emotions and speech. I consoled him and advised him to just be faithful to me and our friendship so I forgave him. So, we moved on.

Months later, he committed the same cheating so I decided to confront him again, but this time I wanted out. I had never seen a man cry and go mad literally so much that he nearly got knocked down by a car. I helped him home and we went off to sleep in our own spaces. So many incidents after the other happened. We went through many break ups but we still sustained the friendship and lived and visited each other just like partners would do. Though Mills was working, his salary was not forthcoming because of the many loans he had contracted which got deducted at source. I kept him through all these financial stresses and supported him greatly; from him to his mum to his siblings and extended family. Mills had two sons but was divorced and I really supported him in all aspects. I felt happy doing so because I had made my mind it was help I was giving and nothing else. When Mills got money, we used it as well. We were happy and no one complained. We knew how to manage when there was no money, but Mills I must say did not know how to manage much. No wonder he was in deep financial crisis when I met him. We bought gifts for each other. We bought clothes, shoes, iPad, phones and many more. Most came from me though, but I never complained. Mills used to receive cash transfers from some guys abroad and helped cushion him. But in all these, Mills never stopped his cheating and lies. He never stopped his deceptions of sticking to me alone. I knew he lied but I continued to try to help him change. I had come to like and treat him as my bother more than partner. Being a few years older too, I tried to use my seniority to advise him all the time; some he took and others I never saw any tangible and practical execution of. In all, Mills was a nice and free-spirited person, but my problem was he was well-known in the gay community. Because of his dick, I think. Gay bottom guys love big, dicks either long or thick or both. So I guess he was hot cake so to say. I tried taming his outings which worked. We were all good until one fine day.

The final straw which broke the camel's back was when he had lied to me of a friend visiting him from the United Kingdom. He only told me he was coming on holiday and was just going to help him navigate his way 'round. I advised and gave him more leads to help. It was later he told me his friend had been visiting from time to time. Then I began to be suspicious. I tried fishing out the lies and tricks. During his friend's stay, Mills moved in with him and did everything with the friend as partners. He kept me informed about some of the things. He told me he had nothing to hide and was just helping him, but I also realised this strange friend-partner of his bought him gifts, goodies and went out with him to night clubs and even with the son. In fact, they were living as partners, but he kept telling me nothing was happening between them.

*So in the gay world, a gay person can visit another gay friend, stay with each other in the same room, eat together, drink together, bath together, sleep on the same bed, go out together and nothing would happen?* I asked myself. I confronted Mills but he still insisted nothing had happened. That was the threshold of lies and deceptions I couldn't take anymore. This was because I knew Mills to incline towards where there was cash, would have more sex and enjoy. Hitherto, I was not financially sound so I also thought that was the reason why he did what he did.

While his friend was still in town, I went to visit Mills' auntie and surprisingly, he with his friend visited as well. I could feel the uneasiness and tension so had to quickly leave to prevent us being found out at least. But one thing that struck me more was the fact that Mills introduced his auntie, son and cousin to his friend but was unable to do the same for me. There I knew he had lied to his friend about not having a partner and that was heart-wrenching. So that night, I left with lots of questions bothering me in my mind. I quarrelled on phone with him, but he found some excuse. Another thing that was questionable was the fact that Mills never called me or was he not able to talk freely while with his friend.

I decided to finally do a litmus test to clear the doubts. So I sat down to draft some questions to ask him when we would meet. I informed him I wanted us to meet and talk while his friend was here, but he insisted I wait till he was gone.

Now the litmus test was for him to invite me to meet his friend and conveniently introduce me to him as his partner. Then I would know if he could do that and I could also ascertain at first hand his friend's reaction. I asked for such a meeting because I also envisaged it would offer an opportunity to find out from his friend who he really was to Mills. If they were just friends wanting to be partners or just mature adults having fun. I had planned to also confront some issues if the friend was not what he had told me, but in a decent way. I had planned to also befriend him so as to maintain future contact and know what exactly was going on or likely to go on in the future. I was sure of knowing these because as a white person, gayism was no news and no illegality surrounded the open professing and I was sure he wasn't going to lie either. But I also told myself of the possibility of meeting a crooked person as well.

The introduction was delayed. I asked Mills why he had delayed it but he told me he had told his friend about me and as such the introduction had already been made. That was the most absurd statement I had heard. How on earth can one be introduced to another person without both being around? There is a great disparity between introduction and telling someone about another. Mills had done it again, trying to be smart, but I vowed to hold a meeting to finally decide the way forward with Mills. We agreed on a meeting day, time and place to extensively discuss issues. I made it clear of knowing he had been lying to me. However, upon careful consideration, I called the meeting off. But I managed to siphon some information from Mills. He actually had gotten involved with this guy for some reasons. Foremost of them was to receive some help in the form of material stuff and money. Second was to lead this guy on to help him travel outside his home country. I pondered over such reasons only to conclude Mills was ever ready to do anything for money, materials and travel. That was the case I was unable to provide, and I now became aware he was going to look elsewhere. That is how relationships are. They come with all the lies and self-centredness. They come with the bad, the ugly and the good.

Relationships, be it same sex or opposite sex, come with the expected and unexpected. There is nothing like a perfect relationship, a little cheat here and a little truthfulness there. That is what Mills handed over to me. The truth is, I loved Mills because he was caring and loving by all standards, but my problem was he was too vulnerable and easily convinced when it came to love. He was the one that couldn't be trusted all 'round. I learned to live with some of his cheatings and still enjoyed him. That was all I could do as I didn't want to be jumping from one to the other. It was that I accepted his cheating based on anything. I just loved him and knew my relationship wasn't going to be forever should he continue that way. I also realised he easily fell in love and it was really risky to trust him. So I never did. We were lovers, brothers and friends and that kept us going. I still get in touch with him for fun. It is funny how we both think we love each other and are still in love, but Mills wasn't fully committed. I have always been committed and I know it won't be long that we will end it all together. So the world goes on. I have loved, continue to love and will love until such a time I will not love anymore. I know it was going to end but didn't know when, how, where, when and what the prevailing conditions would be. So I forge on and live to see. I just couldn't bring myself to think we were going to be forever. If it be so, I would willingly embrace it though. That was how it all went with Mills.

On hearing George's narration about Mills, it was clearly evident that the relationship still lurked in the shadows and any light shining on it was going to bring it to life. It was my duty as a counsellor to help him break such a relationship of the same sex if he really and truthfully wanted out.

# Chapter Seven

# London

Frantic preparation went on as I put finishing touches to my travel to London. I knew I was going to study, but I also knew everything is allowed when it comes to sex in London and that alone made me happy. I, being the adventurous type and will go for anything that gives me satisfaction and happiness, had well prepared my mind and myself.

I had worked a year as an intern and another year with a prestigious airline company after school. I had to put in my resignation to allow me leave and in good faith. This I did and my boss even wished me well and told me I was always be welcomed back.

Because I worked with an airline, I had long reserved my flight. It was scheduled and I couldn't tell many friends. After school, there was a frantic pressure on many of us to break through the job market and it was competition as usual. We found our paths. Some created their paths while others joined the paths of already established ones. I was wondering how London was all going to be. I quizzed my mind about the people, the culture, the school, the language and many things. It was a new world for me and I had planned to take the full opportunity should any arise. Before I went to London, I had a fair idea because I had researched. I knew a lot of things before going, but it would be the first time to experience what I knew from books.

I checked in at the only international airport in Ghana, the Kotoka International Airport, much earlier because I hated surprises springing up on me. No one went to see me off. I was the daring type. But on the departure floor, I saw many people who hugged, kissed and waved at their relatives and loved ones to bid them a safe trip. I never had anyone because I had intended it to be so.

The airport to me was bustling with all seriousness and many activities. It was all business as usual. I realised this was not my first time travelling abroad, but I always have not considered going to South Africa as one until I met people who were travelling to South Africa and it was a big thing for them. In South Africa, travelling to Ghana was a big thing because South Africans are not the travelling type.

A few moments later, the Tannoy system within the airport announced my flight details and drew closer to go through a designated check point before entering my flight and taking my seat close to the window. This time, I was not sitting in the aisles.

A flight attendant helped me fix my hand luggage, took me to my seat and waited. After every traveling passenger was on board, there was the normal drill they took people through. The plane raced the tarmac and minutes later, we were airborne. I sat tightly as I counted the six hours in decreasing order. I couldn't wait for my cousin to meet me at the Heathrow Airport. This was Robert, my cousin that I loved a lot. He had travelled there earlier on work study visa and now was in the Royal Armed Forces. I was going to be with him and nostalgic moments came to mind, but again I fought the whole idea in my mind as I didn't want anything to do with a brother again. It is called incest. At least, my early church days had exposed me to the demonic nature of incest and also sex with animals. In fact, the church condemned all forms of sex apart from the one between man and woman. Even that there was a clause and that sex was to be amongst a married man and a married woman. Anything aside that was evil. For me, all the evils rested on me because I had gone beyond and beyond.

Heathrow Airport per my judgment put Kotoka in the shade as an airstrip. Heathrow was big with five terminals as compared to Kotoka's only one terminal. Robert waited for me outside at the arrival lounge. I finally went through immigration check points and now the whole of London was in front of me. Robert had arranged a bus and it was all enlightening and fun. We talked about many things except for what had happened between us some time ago when we were teenagers.

We got home and I was ushered in and welcomed. I was shown a room to lodge in. I learned I was going to share the room with Robert. I had a meal and sat down as we talked and talked till it was late. I took a warm shower and went to sleep. I dreaded what would happen in the night but thanks to change of mind, nothing as I was thinking happened. I must say, I was happy because I really fought this whole same-sex affair. There were times I wished to do that and times that I did not want to.

I had travelled earlier than the reopening date so I had a few days to wander around. Robert was busy so I did the sightseeing and getting to know London all by myself. I got to know some places of interest to me. I noticed pubs, night clubs, recreational centres and planned on enjoying myself here.

All went as planned as the days unfolded. I went to school and did my enrolment. London Imperial College was a spectacle, more cosmopolitan and very welcoming. I got a hostel near campus for a cheaper rate but after two months checked out as I had found a lady friend who I stayed with.

I moved in as an ordinary friend and it was her intelligence that attracted me to her. We shared something in common, but she was a mixed-race pretty girl with a Jamaican descent. By this, I realised I was more attracted to fairer ladies. We co-existed without a problem. Over time, we shared the bills which made it easier for both of us. We all had one aim and that was to make the grades and pass well. We also happened to have attended some lectures together. My stay with Lena marked a turning point which got me attracted to ladies, but she remained a platonic friend. I had few lady friends on campus. We had short flings here and there, but I wasn't committed to anyone. Due to my sexual activities, I thought I was addicted to sex until I was explained to that I was only being too sexually active and boisterous. I got worried sometimes because I really had a very active sexual life. First semester on campus was all about settling and limited my outings but I never fell behind though.

Over time, I came to know about all the good night clubs because I loved music and outing. I also came to know about all the good saunas and steam rooms close to me, even gay ones as well. I was restricted when I was with Lena and it was good for me. But soon, I was going to bounce back in full swing doing what I did best with men and women. For me, sex with the same gender was a choice and not a compulsion or my make-up. I didn't want to live in denial. I always decided to have sex or not. I am in no way condemning gays who claim they were born as such but I beg to differ. I believe gayism is a learned behaviour. It is a choice like other behaviours. One can choose to stay in that habit or leave it. I cannot hold brief for any gay, but for me it was a choice. In all my gay life, I never wanted to regret anything so I must say I had an alert mind and made choices. No one compelled me.

I looked out for all the gay joints in and around me. I even toured their site online and I couldn't believe London was that liberal to homosexuals. It was a free city and, for that matter, a free United Kingdom. I once passed by two male guys kissing right on the street and thought I was dreaming only to open my eyes to their lips still glued together. I told myself this was a very bad place because where I come from, we did not need to be sensually and sexually exposed and tagged.

# Chapter Eight

## London Lifestyle

"Counsellor!" George called, exclaiming.

This time, George took a deep sigh and told me he would be more graphical here because London was where the whole problems started.

In London, my first place of call was Chariots at Streatham in South-West London. I got to know chariots as a brand name had four of such facilities and had planned to experience them one after the other.

On my first day at Streatham, I felt bad going in there so I went in the evening, trying to hide from the full glare of the public. Unfortunately, it was located right in front of a bus stop. I hovered around till I saw no one coming and I quickly dashed in. The whole place was locked up so I rang a bell and a topless receptionist surfaced. He said it cost eight pounds. Oh, I didn't know it was a paid facility, but all the same paid and entered as he gave me two towels. For a moment, I sat in the changing area and contemplated a while. I still couldn't understand why I was in there. I was wondering what I should wear. Obviously, I had a towel to use when I was done. Then I saw a guy pass by in towel like he was going to the bathhouse. I grabbed a locker and changed, putting the towel around my waist. I locked all my stuff in a locker and held on to the key. The lockers were coin-operated and had to slot one pound which was retrievable when one was leaving the facility.

I took a tour 'round the place. It had two sauna cabins, a steam room, a large bubbly spa pool and a host of rest rooms for use. Once I paid at the reception, I got entitled to use all the facilities. The place had satellite television lounge, a snack bar and free Wi-Fi once I was in there but had to pay for any snack I took. I moved 'round and inspected the place. I saw condoms placed at vantage points along with some lubes. I still was deep in thought what all these were for. I checked in some rooms and the television beamed some gay porn.

*So this whole place is meant for gay sex?* I asked myself rhetorically. Of course, no one was at hand to answer anyway.

My tour was not without the stare and looks from those already in, I guessed they knew I was new there because my bewilderment might have owned me up. But I quickly adjusted and blended in, so I headed straight to the showers and hung up my towel. This time, I wasn't worried much because people felt free to show off their body and I guess anyone that didn't want to show off his body might as well not have paid to enter. There few guys around the place and the stares were too much when a white hunk approached, commending me for my nice body. This was the first time a guy had said that to me in a sensual way so I thought, hang on, a lot of ladies had said that before but this time it had come from a guy. I felt good. He came close as if examining me from head to toe. He passed so many comments, but the ones that stuck to mind were, "nice butts", "nice body" and "perfect dick". This time, I was getting aroused so I grabbed my towel and wrapped it around my waist. This guy still followed me wherever I went. I decided to go into the sauna for the first time in my life.

A dry heat welcomed me. The room was romantically lit with some red and dim bulbs. Few guys sat enjoying the heat as if it was no one's business. Most eyes were wide opened when I entered and the stares continued. I reached for a part of the bench in the far corner. I exchanged few pleasantries and sat quietly. The guy who I had met in the showers also came in and was looking for me, I could tell. He told me he was mesmerised by my figure, built and niceness so wanted a piece of me. It sounded bullyish to me. All the same, he settled down and tried to reach for my penis from under my towel but I prevented him. He tried again and again till I couldn't take it anymore and left the sauna for the steam room. He followed me there again. This time, we were all alone. He reached for my penis, massaging me all over and then bent down to give me a blowjob. I felt some pin sensation under my feet which wasn't good at all so I moved my penis from his mouth and pushed away, and went off to the other side of the steam room. He came towards me, grabbed my hand and started sucking my nipples and licking my body all over.

*Is that how it works here?* I asked myself rhetorically.

He continued and sucked me till I came in his mouth and for the first time, I witnessed someone swallowing my sperm. He seemed to enjoy it. He sucked me again and again, saying my dick was delicious. For a moment, I realised my penis was bigger than his. I hadn't taken cognisance of this, but with my encounter over time with many people, I came to appreciate I was well-endowed. Having some nine inches long and six inches thick penis was in the least a little cock at all.

That night was lovely, but I went to shower and quickly left the premise. I stood outside in the cold waiting for a bus home. I loved everything and planned going back again. But as I was leaving, I picked a flyer along. I read it and realise they had four branches and decided to visit all of them since they all were located at different places. The nearest was the Streatham facility, then Waterloo, Vauxhall and Shoreditch. I got fascinated about these places as I continued going to Streatham almost every weekend. I met many people over and over again. Most of them were whites, with a few Latinos. Occasionally, some blacks came too.

The first black guy I met there was Mada, a naturalised Southern African from Malawi. He had a huge dick compared to mine. Another time, I met this Nigerian called Vincent, whose dick was very huge that I measured some thirteen inches. We became friends and I visited him at times at his residence at Clapham Junction where we always had sex. He loved me penetrating him and would give me some few quid when we were done. I didn't understand why he would give me money, but I accepted it all the same. Vincent arranged a meeting where I met another Jamaican called CJ who adored me so much. That night, I did a double work having sex with both. After my rounds, CJ also penetrated Vincent and I realised they were friends and with Vincent's dick, I wondered who he could penetrate so he was always on the receiving side. His dick was thick and long that it took time to harden up and when it did, it easily became soft. I had read a few times that there were those who had monster dicks that they needed more blood to pump into the veins of the shaft of the penis to be erected and kept erected. I think Vincent had a dysfunctional erection as he couldn't sustain his erection for long and took him a long time to get hard. Even with that, it felt soft. He really needed a medical check-up, I thought it over in my mind. He was heavily endowed for sure in length and thickness. CJ tried to bounce on me after he finished with Vincent, but I didn't agree. I had not been penetrated before and I didn't intend to allow anyone to thrust their dick into me; I had read some side effects and didn't want to think about even trying. We had a nice time all naked around the apartment, took some drinks and we caressed each other while Vincent this time had put on a porn film for us to watch. That was my first time of having a threesome. I had heard of it, but this time I was experiencing it.

Even in threesome, one realises the inclination towards a particular person. If care is not taken in threesome, it will become two. That is, when one is side-lined due to the body chemistry two out of the three may have towards each other. In a threesome, the third side-lined person makes the effort to get into the play or will be more isolated. It all has to do with the mind, which one gravitates towards more, the liking, the submissiveness and the flow from the experience.

That evening at home, I lay in bed reminiscing all that had gone on and something in me wanted more. It was the sexual animal in me calling for more. My dick stayed stiff for a long time as I kept thinking about what had transpired. It is the same in sex with anyone; your mind gets prepared and fixated on having sex with someone before you even start. In the cases where there has not been a thought through or mind fixation, it becomes a bit hard in the first instance until such a time one gets in the groove. I have come to understand and believe sex is a mind game which must be played by people of sound minds.

My next stop was going to be the Waterloo facility which I got to know was the United Kingdom's largest sauna. It had a steam room that could accommodate forty men, a video lounge like in Streatham, the whole place was fully air-conditioned, Internet-facilitated suites and paying snack bars. Indeed, it was big. I found out and got to know it covered some five thousand square feet. That was a big space for that matter. This was going to be my next. Waterloo put Streatham in the shade. I envisaged there would be more people there too.

This went on for a while as I also attended church and church choir meetings. It was right after choir meeting that I would visit my Chariots, stayed for a while and went home late, only to wake up early for church. Most times, I would minister at church because of my nice voice. That I know because I know. In fact, my pastor even confirmed it. I attended two churches and sung in both.

I came to confirm that because one sings at church does not make one holy or spiritual. In fact, one can still have the gift of singing but the glory of God might have long departed from you. The anticipated presence of God may not be there but the theatrics and performance will be there to wow the audience. It was a total deception. I knew I had a problem but my church folks applauded me so much so that I was lost in these fine words to realise the other side I was battling with.

I planned with Mada to visit Waterloo, to which he obliged. The place was really huge and had a lot of people that night. I went through the reception as usual, got my towels and then went straight to the changing rooms. The place was very busy. The looks on the faces were of men expecting something. They came across as grey hounds sniffing a prey to attack. That is they come prying around, then prey on their victim. Mada and I sat to chat for a long time. I wanted to find out why he was into the same-sex affair, but seriously I was appalled by his answer. For him, he wanted his papers to stay in the United Kingdom so had gone into what they called Civil Partnership with a gay guy who had documents to stay in the United Kingdom so his papers could and would cover him. He asked me if I would do the same, but I responded negatively. After all, I was only a student and my papers were okay.

That night, I couldn't believe what I saw. The rest rooms were all full and filled up. Some were lurking in the wings waiting for others to come out so they could also enter. One area that intrigued me was a cubicle where one would push his dick through a round hole and not knowing who was waiting in the other cubicle, you got sucked. Many a time after one's blowjob session, you may want to meet the fellow and sometimes exchange numbers. That was how people made friends and kept contacts. I tried it, but never bothered to know who had given me the blowjob. All the time, I stayed with Mada. We passed by a crowded place, and this time it was sex orgy. Many people surrounded two people having sex, watched, waited and took turns. It wasn't rape, but I saw it as agreed rape; there being many of such instances happening around. People seemed enthused and patiently fondled one another as they waited. I thought the one being penetrated must be strong because the men waiting were many. Some used condoms, others sexed raw.

This is where it becomes dangerous for group sex, especially when you go raw. The viruses lurk around and move from one person to another through semen. It is amazing how sexual pleasure makes people forget about protection altogether. Once a raw fucker pulls out, I stood and saw another person penetrate unprotected. I thought and asked if they knew about sexually transmitted diseases, or they were insulated against them, or just didn't bother. I did that wearing double condoms. I just didn't want to take chances. Life is good and too short to be saddled with unwanted diseases or diseases hitherto could have been prevented. That would be foolishness in the highest order.

I parted with Mada and the next time I saw him, he was being battered by some group of guys. He saw me but showed no concern. I jumped on from behind him unknowingly and gave him a good round of show. He turned to see what that was and locked into an eye contact with me. He beckoned and I went another round. I did justice to him and after that, we both went to the steam room. He confessed to me I really fucked him well and would love another. Our meeting kept on being based on sex. He lived at Woking and would travel to London each time or occasionally I visited him.

By this time, I decided to purchase more porn materials so I could see and learn different sex positions and also know how to use the sex apparatuses.

I once witnessed a guy who was held in the air by four able-bodied men while he was penetrated from mid-air by a fifth person while another squatted to suck his dick. Obviously, that demanded strength. After each round of sex, they exchanged positions so they all had their turns. All this happened in the gay saunas or at times at organised gay parties. It was very discreet when it was done at parties, but in saunas, it was a field day to meet and try any rough sex anyone wanted. It was as if people had learned the sex theory and the sauna and steam were the practical rooms or places to unleash what had learned.

In fact, after my rounds with Mada, I left to relax in the lounge, watching a video. I waited for him as he still sought for more sex. When he was done, we left. I asked him how it felt to be fucked that hard. He was the only person I could ask and he was very frank with me. He told me if it was the first, it was very unpleasant but with time as he described it, when you get opened up, you can then manage the manoeuvrings behind as you get thrusting in and out. He admitted it was always painful but after the penetration, it was all right. I saw him off at Waterloo Train Station and continued home.

I decided to visit Chariots Vauxhall alone the next time. This time, I went during the week day during one of my off days. All this time, as I indulged in these sexual escapades, I was also afraid and feared to be found out by people I knew. I went through the reception and on the doorway was CJ. Well, for him I didn't mind. I got the shock of my life when I chanced upon a university mate named Kwame. At first, we gazed at each other and the next question I heard was what you are doing here. I shrugged it off and posed the same. I felt shy, but he felt happy. He dragged me along quite surprised. He then told me he never ever suspected I was bisexual. I asked what that was. He told me it meant you are interested in both men and women. He surely knew my girlfriend then so he was right and spot on. The facility was huge. It happened to be the United Kingdom's busiest and largest sauna as it boasted of two-thirty saunas, hot spa pool, two steam rooms, two video lounges, a five-hundred lockers changing room, Internet suite, snack bars and numerous rest rooms. This facility was only some three minutes from the Vauxhall Station. I felt very much uncomfortable as Kwame waited for me to change. He pulled me and seemed to be a regular customer there. It was my first time and he noticed it. It gave me some leverage as I tried to explain it was my first time. Kwame was all over the place. I was wondering what people around thought of us moving together and checking into a rest room. Kwame was all into it and asked what I wanted to do.

"Nothing," I responded.

He took off my towel as he pulled his off too. He had a

small dick. It was too small for his stature. In the end, we had a good time having sex in different positions. He gave a blowjob and for the first time, it was nasty as he lifted my butts with my back down and licked my ass. He tried using his tongue to penetrate my ass. It felt ticklish and easily got me aroused. I don't remember how many rounds of sex we had but Kwame knew how to keep his man busy. And each time I got aroused, he would slip my penis into his ass. This meant that he was please do the job. After that, he would lick my earlobes playing with them, then my nipples as usual. He had a way of sucking my dick just on the top part that's the head as if it was a lollipop. He took me to another level. I realised he had been in this for a long time and really knew his stuff. He told me at times in the facility he got fucked and they paid him. I blatantly told him that was male or gay prostitution. He would not have any of my nonsense, he said, and continued his love-making. He knew what he wanted and knew how to arouse a guy.

We stayed together the whole day till it was evening. We rested, took some snacks which he bought and then enjoyed the hot spa pool before we left the place. We exchanged numbers since he also told me he had not been fucked that good, nice and many times like that before. He praised me of having horse strength and that was how he liked his men. It was flattering for a male counterpart to sing those praises. Out meetings went on even at odd hours when he visited me at work. We would quickly dash to the male washroom for a quickie. The slightest free time was an opportunity we had. He wasn't far from where I lived but I didn't want to entertain him much should any known person spot the two of us. He had come out as a gay and never was discreet. This I feared for him but he told me he wasn't going to marry but all this while, I was also planning a marriage.

Kwame didn't mind me going raw. Even when I tried wearing a condom, he objected, saying it was never the same as going raw. "That's how you feel the flesh," he said. This went on for quite a long time. He became my ready and regular sex partner. I called him each time I felt like I wanted to have sex and he never missed out. He even proposed to me that we get into a relationship, but I watered down that idea. It was something I never liked. I also met a few of Kwame's friends.

For the first time, I felt sick and my general practitioner, GP, told me I had contracted some sexually transmitted disease, STD, but assured me it was curable and advised I use condoms. He did not know I got it through homosexuality. In London, one dared not look down on anyone since every sex form was acceptable, for all I know and have read and witnessed. He prescribed some drugs for me which I fetched from Superdrug. It was bad going to buy the drug. Of course, the pharmacist knew she was giving me drugs to cure an STD. She told me to contact her if I didn't understand anything. This was going to lead to another relationship. I always wished to marry a white lady and it was great for me.

I had a long and nice relationship with this pharmacist from Superdrug. It all started from her offering help and stopped at us being together. I loved her so much. She was caring and thoughtful. We had our own moments of good and bad. I even went to the extent of knowing the family, but it was not to be. We fell off after three years with a child between us.

My boy is still in London and I visit every time I am there. We fell apart because Aileen got to know I was a bi-sexual. She thought I could change and we would tie the knot. I also thought the same. But that never was to be.

## Poppers

The last Chariots place was the Shoreditch facility. It was enormous and was the largest of all the four saunas I had visited. It covered some twenty thousand square feet with the biggest and fabulous heated pool of twenty by forty feet in size, two hot spa pools, two large saunas, two steam rooms, a large spacious warm room, television lounges, snack bar, a heated smoking area, Internet suite, fully equipped gym, qualified masseur services, some five hundred locker changing rooms and a free big car park for clients. The place was nice and just a stone throw from Liverpool Street Station. There was a lot one could do in there. It came with all recreational facilities for free except for the masseur services and the snack bar. I went to the place alone. I always did that so I do not get pressured by anyone and that allowed me to inspect and tour the place at my own leisure and enjoyed as and when. I could afford to also leave at any time too. There was the usual reception protocol but what I realised was this time, it cost me fifteen pounds. I am sure all the facilities were included in the charge. All the same it was a cool fifteen quid to get to use all these. Most often, one cannot access all of them. I took my usual tour straight to gym and met a few guys exercising. I got onto a treadmill and started my own thing. I moved from one puller to another resistant machine. Some guys were in the gym area only to feast their eyes on the hunks that trooped in there. I don't brag to have a nice physique, but I knew then I had it and most people liked my physique. The first person to chat me up in the gym was this cute-looking Indian called Raju. He was extra nice, but he came across too feminine for my liking. He just couldn't leave my side and followed me everywhere I went. He went for two bottles of orange-flavoured Lucozade and gave me one. At one point, I felt too cornered as he would not leave my side. He signalled me to follow him and we locked ourselves in one of the rest rooms. The rest rooms were partitioned with some see-through wood so the next person could see all that one did in the other. It wasn't like that for all, but we found ourselves in one of those. Raju rubbed his hands over my well-chiselled chest whispering some words I could barely hear, but I thought he was admiring my masculinity. He opened his mouth and told me to fuck it. He tried swallowing my dick deep down and just when he began choking, he released it. He continued for several times. It was a form of blowjob but he literally would engulf my whole dick in his mouth. For the first time, fucking the mouth was interesting. He pulled a small bottle, opened it and inhaled some. I asked what it was. But he was too busy with my dick in his mouth, he couldn't answer, so I picked the bottle and saw an inscription; 'Poppers'. It was some form of a tranquiliser, I imagined. He was aggressive with me after inhaling the poppers. I fucked his mouth and spilled the sperm on his face and he smeared it over his body as well. He became restless and clinched to me, begging me to penetrate him. At this point, a few guys had gathered to watch us as if we were on set for a porn movie. Some tried to put their hands through the wooden partition but we were well adjusted in one corner so they couldn't touch us. The noise Raju made had attracted them. By now, there were a lot more and they squeezed themselves to catch a glimpse of what was going on. Some shouted some jargons I wasn't familiar with but again I thought they were cheering me up. Jargons like "Roast him", "Tear him up", "Full penetration", "Pound him" among other came across to us. I didn't take notice of them much as I tore a lube which was water-based and smeared it down his ass to allow easy penetration as he craved to have me inside him. He had a very tight ass but the lubes helped a great deal. I fully penetrated him and a loud noise of approval came from those watching. I pounded him hard and he told me to inhale some of the poppers. I did and it gave me some extra strength, an instant energy of aggression. I fucked him real hard and for a long time. I lost count how many rounds I came. I also didn't mind if these onlookers had cameras or not. I was just engrossed in the sex. Finally, I got exhausted and pulled out. Raju still wanted me to continue, but by this time I needed to relax and regain some strength. It took more than one hour with him in that rest room. People still looked on. I opened the door and more people came in, but I left to take a shower downstairs. I strolled around a bit and came back to see Raju still being roasted in the rest room. This was my first time I saw a person being fucked continuously for more than two hours. It was a pathetic scene, but he seemed to be enjoying it by allowing others to jump on him. His body was so slender and feminine and behaved also as such. It was like free sex and everyone pounced on him. I felt sorry for him because I didn't know whether the noise he made was a normal thing, he kept groaning but would occasionally ask them to fuck him hard.

I spent more hours there than any place I had visited before. The place was large and had a lot to offer also. Raju finally left the room and went to wash down all the sperm they smeared over him. He looked awful and sort of tired when he was going. I heard some jerks of laughter from the guys who had enjoyed him. I heard some say "Go home to mama", "Do you want more?", "We will be waiting here for you, sugar" among others. They actually didn't care once one gave himself up. At one time, too much going on as I saw a huge man thrusting in and out of him and would occasionally whip him, another bouncing his dick on his face and occasionally would choke him with his uncut dick, someone sucked his nipples and another played with his dick. They totally utilised and roasted him.

Raju sauntered down the stairs to the showers. I could see he was tired as his walking changed as well. The next time I saw him, he was sleeping or relaxing in the television lounge. He must have been seriously tired. I cannot describe fully what was done to him by the other guys, but some enjoyed inflicting pain on their sex victims. There was this guy who, as he pounded Raju, whacked him all the time. One could hear his slaps as he whacked him. I wondered if he enjoyed the whole adventure. This is termed as master and slave sex. Some used different gadgets, whips, leather belts, chains and saddles for sex pleasures.

**Masseuse Services**

Since I had not been massaged before, I took the opportunity to try it. I walked into the massage room after resting enough. He asked me to pay I think ten pounds as he started setting the place up. There were two guys in there. All this time, I had my towel 'round my waist. One asked what type of service I wanted. I just wanted massage. I was told to lie on the neatly laid hospital-like bed, face-down. I did it and the next moment I could feel some oils on my body and hands all over me. The skills with which they massaged were great. He managed my whole body from my neck region to my toes. I really was hard this time. After a long massage at my back, he told me to turn over only for him to see my huge dick dangling and breathing as it jerked up and down.

He laughed and said, "Naughty boy."

By his intonation, I knew he was Spanish. There was pre-cum dripping down my penis, so he skilfully wiped it off with another towel and started another massage. I asked his name and he replied as Rafael.

He said, "I like you, that's why I told you my name."

His other partner looked on, supplying him with whatever he asked for during the massage. Soon I was done and he acted so professionally and gave me a complimentary card to call if I ever needed a massage. I thanked them and left.

By this time, I didn't want to get involved so I went to lie in the Jacuzzi and enjoyed the bubbles and the massage they created. I closed my eyes and relaxed, but I could feel some movement under water, a hand trying to grab my dick. Of course, I wasn't alone in there. This fine fat white guy pulled closer and played with my dick in the water. He whispered to me, asking if I would fuck him. At the same time, there was this Somalian guy also in the Jacuzzi who pulled closer as well. They both left the Jacuzzi at the same time, giving me some eye contact to follow them. I went after them and into this all dark rest room. The Somalian introduced himself as Tesfaye working at duty free shop at Stanstead Airport. They both were big in nature with some protruding bellies. I didn't want to do much, but allowed them to suck me in turns and played with my nipples and balls. They insisted I penetrate them, but I refused. Little did I know what was to follow!

## Sex for Cash

Tesfaye told me to penetrate him and he would pay me. I had not encountered any such offer before, so I obliged. He told me to hold on as he tried to penetrate his friend and later told me to also penetrate him. So it was like double penetration. I fucked from behind as he also fucked his friend. It was a novelty and wasn't that enjoying but I continued for the money he had promised me. We finished quickly because I really wasn't into big guys. Tesfaye went down and got me fifty pounds. He took my contact and promised to call and that he wanted us to be friends. He told me he would pay me each time we had an affair and would also bring me free designer perfumes. It sounded good. That day at Shoreditch really was a memorable one. I did so many different things.

When I was about to leave, I went down to the television lounge to wake up Raju. He was already up when I went and smiled. I told him I was leaving, but he wanted me to stay. I couldn't stay any longer because my course work was to be completed, so we exchanged numbers and I checked out that day. I still remember my first day with fond memories.

## Graduating

I completed my course work as was required and finally graduated after one full year of intense master's programme. It was fun and good to put academics behind to find work this time. One person I was going to miss was Lena, who had really encouraged and helped me. I finally graduated on one solemn Friday afternoon with the best of grades. I was the overall best student once again. During that graduation, we had the opportunity to meet and interact with some of the finest business fraternity in London. It was great and I did well to mingle, taking advantage of every opportunity.

## Amsterdam

After school, I wanted to continue for a doctoral programme so I took a job that was less stressful to enable me to do so. I took an offer as a librarian at Imperial College and also a part-time at the weekends as a gym instructor at Brixton Recreational Centre, The Rec as they called it. The combination worked perfectly as I prepared to enrol for my doctorate. The cost was so high; I needed to work double to save enough.

My work as a librarian wasn't fun at all since it was demanding, but all the same I was up to the task. The part-time job at the Rec was fun as I met all manner of people; workers, students, high class and all levels of people.

At the Rec, which is a six-floor recreational facility, a lot went on, but they never entertained sex on their premises. As much as they couldn't stop anyone; be it gay, bisexual or heterosexual, it was a known fact that almost everyone that visited the place was straight. Or better still, they lied to themselves to believed so because at least CJ was a constant attendant and knew what he wanted. I never liked working at the Rec because there had been too many violent cases. I worked for one full year and left.

While there, I met Frank, a Nigerian I helped by accommodating him for a while and later found out he was gay. He decided to go into civil partnership to regularise himself which was his own decision. We became good buddies, but he never got to know I was attracted to him. He was a gym freak and had a nice contoured physique but nothing happened between us.

At one time, CJ approached me and asked that we go to Amsterdam for a carnival. It sounded good. There were cheap flights by many airlines. It was going to be a weekend away. I welcomed the idea. We booked our hotels for two days, and were going to be gone for three days; that is, going on Friday and returning on Sunday. I didn't know the nitty gritty of the carnival but was all up for it.

I wasn't bothered much because CJ was a regular attendant to these carnivals. He had informed me on Tuesday and we had to go on the following Friday, so I quickly put in some strange off-duty excuse which was not easy to be granted. As a student, I applied for a tourist visa which was a same-day service. We made our way to London City Airport and from there to Amsterdam's Schiphol Airport. It was a quick flight. On the plane, CJ told me it was a carnival that was organised every year with different cultures and people attending. He made it clear it was a gay pride movement but was enjoyed by all. I asked many question and he answered all of them.

We soon landed, checked out of the airport to our booked hotel. Our hotel was just along the Amstel river which housed some three hundred or more brothels, gay pubs and other sex places. This place was called Red Light District. In fact, at night, the whole place looked red with those red lightings. I got to know that Amsterdam's Red Light District was a carnival place, full of all the vices one could think of; from prostitution, drugs to human trafficking. Popular scenes were skimpily dressed prostitutes in brothels with glass windows, strip tease clubs, coffee shops and controversial mind boggling museums. The Red Light District was locally termed De Wallen which was just around the Central Station, around the neon-lit Canals Oudezijds Voorburgwal and Oudezijds Achterburgwal. Where the carnival was more concentrated was at Warmoesstraat which was Red Light District's main gay action area. The place was bustling with cruises, houseboats trips, carnal houses and festivals. It was a sight to behold. It was rich cultural experience with wonderful carnival dresses. Most gays wore some feminine dress or were topless, especially the muscled guys.

CJ and I went into a popular coffee shop named Greenhouse. We sat for a while and enjoyed the scenery. It was whole new experience as the people that trooped to the Red Light District were uncountable. I was lost totally but followed

CJ as he led the way like in a maze. It was going to be a long night for us. Prostitutes beckoned from their windows and shops but we passed. All I wanted to find was what we actually came to do. On reaching Warmoesstraat, I was now convinced why they always said it was the gay capital of the world. Anything and everything was going on. I cannot describe in depth, but it was a sight to behold. Some men got laid right in the public place, but discreetly. Of course, it was night and dim so they hid at shady corners from the full glare of the public but you would know for sure something was happening. Some kissed on their way as they walked along. There were people holding others and having beers in their hands. I never took. It was a love scene of gays, but what I liked most was the food and music because for sex I had had enough, I told myself. CJ really knew his way around.

We bumped into a guy who introduced himself as Van and only spoke Dutch. I never understood Dutch, neither did CJ, but we managed to chat with signs and the little English he knew. Later in the night, we retired to our room with Van. I was a bit tired but CJ and Van were so much into each other. For once, I wasn't interested; after all, we had Saturday and Sunday to go as well. They really were happy as CJ sucked him and vice versa. They both fucked each other. I witnessed everything but couldn't be drawn into it as I had turned my mind off. We all slept on the same bed that evening. We woke up and again we all took our shower together. We went out and this time it was day and Van led us to many interesting places. We entered a brothel where CJ and I paid for some services. It was fun. Van lived in Amsterdam and didn't find it fascinating. Van waited for us in the brothel's lounge. We met some fine ladies offering us real sex and it was great. They did all the work by riding us and sitting on us as they moved up and down, thrusting their slender bodies over us. Some were voluptuous and nearly suffocated us as they bent over with their heads facing us head-on during sex and kissing. I just wanted to experience these prostitutes and did just that.

Later in the day, we went for lunch at another place called Baba. It was nice food. In the evening, we joined a lot of guys chanting some songs, danced and sampled some of them for our own enjoyment later in our apartment. The whole carnival was interesting only that I hated the fact that they called it gay pride. I never wanted to be tagged as gay, so I didn't like it. We had multiple sex during the carnival. Some guys who came over to our rented apartment had cocaine with them. I was surprised CJ snorted a few lines. Well, I had seen many do it here in Amsterdam these few days we were here but never got involved. They sold it for cheap as well. The business of sex, I realised, came along with drugs, but I was lucky not to have been drawn into drugs. The whole carnival was fun and on Sunday we had to return since I was going to report to work on Monday. I slept at CJ's place that evening upon our return. It wasn't without sex. We had a shower and fucked in there before retiring to bed. I woke up very early and went home to change over for work. The day never passed without me reminiscing what had gone on in Amsterdam. The scenes came to me as flashes and visions. It looked like I was still day dreaming and wished it had never ended. But as all good things end so do bad ones, if at all they were bad.

I got through work without even discussing my trip, but there was this guy who was pestering so much I had to reveal a bit to him. Little did I know he was a bisexual as well. So nothing I said was strange to him, but he had never experienced

Amsterdam before. We agreed the next time we will go together as he was so sorry he did not know of such a carnival. So we agreed for the next and other few outings in and around London.

## Soho and Convent Gardens, London

Some of the friends I met at the saunas called; we met few times and I'm still in touch with some. Notable among them is Tesfaye, because he always brought me perfumes and paid me. We had met many times in my apartment and it was fun. Whenever I visited him, he paid for my transport which was rewarding.

There was also Raju, because he was a sex maniac. We met few times then and continue to meet as and when I want a group sex, where he comes along with few friends of his. Mada too has always been a friend.

One thing was that every new day presented an opportunity to try out a new sex adventure which I did religiously combining my job, my meet ups with friends for sex, my choir rehearsals and church attendance.

I took a stroll one day in Oxford Street for window shopping. I roamed Bond Street and Piccadilly Square till I got to Convent Gardens and Soho. I was amazed at what I saw. It was the first time I saw and got to know that some boxers were made solely for gay guys. The whole place to me was a sex den. There were numerous joints, restaurants, pubs, sex toy shops, pornography shops arrayed with videos and magazines, strip tease clubs, brothels, peeping rooms, cinemas that showed only porn, gay cinemas, saunas, steam rooms, short stay rooms and many more.

I got to know I had a long way to go. I wanted to experience it all and that would call for more money. The place was a sex hub. My first experience here would be to go peeping. This was a place which was coin operated. Once you slotted a pound, the curtains rolled up and naked women teasingly appeared erotically. Every pound slotted was for one minute so the longer you wanted to peep, the more coins you slotted into the machine. There was no contact whatsoever with the naked women. That is why it was called peeping rooms. I dropped a coin and *ta daa* the curtains went up and this naked woman appeared. She wasn't fascinating so I just turned away. She must have been disappointed. I tried another place and stayed for five minutes. Though I stayed for this long, it wasn't amusing at all. I did not see why I should just go watch naked women. This never appealed to me the least and that was to be my first and my last. Since it was day time, there wasn't much I had planned so I went back to return in the evening to experience the night life also. I got back to Oxford Street and took lunch at Chop Stix, a Chinese budget food joint.

Coming back that evening, I was fully prepared to go all out. I met Francis but parted shortly. This place was bustling with activities and certainly was a major part of London life.

Soho was area of the city of Westminster and part of the West End of London. Soho undoubtedly remains the entertainment district with a tag as the centre for the sex industry. Of course, it is a commerce centre and embraces culture and entertainment, but my visit here had been to experience the sex activities. It is known for its risqué vibe and burlesque shows. The whole place is home to many of London's sex shops, gay and lesbian bars. At night, I was overwhelmed by the array of night lives. It was some clubbing, sauna and steam, striptease bars and diners among many others. The place was too much for me to explore. So I decided to take It one after the other.

That evening, I checked into an all-male striptease pub. Most of the guys were topless so I also went topless. There were some hunky guys on stage in g-strings, dancing and manoeuvring in enticing forms. Many of the guys sipped their drinks, others had locked lips, while others massaged the crotches of others. The room was dimly lit and I observed a few around the corners who literally rubbed their crotches behind others like in a dance, but they were in the process of fucking. I got near and could just hear the sex groaning, but no one seemed bothered. I happened to be the only stranger.

I stood for a long time as I watched on and off. Very soon, I got horny and was approached by a very nice hunk. We exchanged pleasantries, took our drinks and, of course, mine was non-alcoholic. He came across as very nice and introduced himself as Zuc. This names still resonates because of what happened after we left the pub. Zuc had informed of living just across the pub in a rented apartment and invited me over that night. He was of Eastern-European descent, but I didn't find out which country. I got to know that because of his accent. We got to his lovely decorated apartment. It wasn't too extravagant but well done. He asked me if I cared for a drink again. To my surprise, a lady brought me the drink. We all sat and enjoy and conversed. Then another guy also came from another room and joined the conversation.

For a moment, I was scared and wanted to leave. I remember on our way up, Zuc had locked many metal gates behind and it set my mind reeling and thinking. I feared for my life, but they were lovely too. The scene came across as a movie

I had watched where murderers entertained their victims well and then killed them. I excused myself to use the wash room. I stayed there for a while and upon returning saw these three housemates seriously in some threesome right in the centre of the living room. By this time, they had pushed the centre table aside and spread some fine woollen blanket on the carpet. Zuc beckoned me to join which I hurriedly did. That night, I saw for the first time what it means when we say masochism and what it was like. On the floor were chains, pins, bandages, plaster, adhesive tapes and rubber strings. They had tied the lady up in both lower and upper limbs. She did not look like she had been forced though. I realised it was all part of the love play. She was happy, but I was afraid for her. I got the chance to fuck her over as Zuc and his friend whipped and whacked her. The whipping to me was intense as they had reddened her skin. At the same time as I fucked her, the other guy tried kissing her and with her lying on her side, I fucked her as he also penetrated her anus at the same time. He was a very huge guy like myself and well-endowed also. So I fucked her pussy as Zuc's friend fucked her ass at the same time. I was on top while he was beneath her. We changed positions as she sat on me to ride and at the same time the other guy penetrated her ass from behind. She could just manage us both. Ladies really can multi-task. We continued, both of us, as we tried reaching orgasms. I pitied the lady but she seemed great and okay. I thought it was something she had been doing with them. We finally came and then they released her.

Zuc held my dick and inserted it in himself. Though I was tired because this was my first time I had fucked a lady with another guy at the same time and that delayed my orgasm. I really didn't find it interesting though. I reached for Zuc's hips, grabbing and holding the ass close my dick as I held it to doggy fuck him on his knees. I did that for a while and just when I was about to cum, he pulled me out and invited his friend. He fucked Zuc for a while and he pulled me close. I did not know what he was trying to do and because his English was poor, he couldn't explain himself so Zuc interjected, saying we both penetrate him at the same time. Wow, I wondered how this was going to be but some way, somehow, following their direction, we both found our dicks fully inserted into Zuc, rubbing each other. I could feel his ass tearing apart but he managed accommodating the two of us. We had turned sideways this time, so obviously we could kiss as well as Zuc lay flat-faced. The lady came close and rubbed some oils on us and played with our scrotums at the same time. This was a whole new way of sex. I loved it and after both of us came, Zuc held our dicks and sprayed his face with our sperms and swallowed some. The other guy then took on the lady using a huge dildo. It was really huge and he inserted the full length of it into her and this time the groaning was intense. It must have been some twenty-inch dildo with about ten to twelve centimetres in width. Zuc sucked her nipples and helped her to orgasm.

The strangest thing I saw was when Zuc got the dildo and literally sat on it with full penetration. His friend reached for adhesive tape to close his mouth as he was shouting and in my bewilderment, I reached to suck his nipples as he himself jerked up and down on it. It was at this point that I realised both of us penetrating him was nothing. Zuc finally ejaculated and spilled it onto her. We performed different sex forms and styles and by the time we finished, it was two in the morning. I was really exhausted and hungry. Zuc and I left them and went back to Convent Gardens to grab a bite. I took his number and we met few times each time I was at Soho. He lived in close proximity to Soho so he became my tour guide in and around.

I was so tired that night so I decided to leave for home but on my way, I passed a gay cinema which attracted me. Just at the corner of the cinema in a somewhat enclosed area, a group of guys had gathered 'round something I couldn't see from afar. I drew near and saw that they had surrounded two guys fucking. There was this fat chap who was being roasted as they termed it and each of the guys who wanted took a turn as and when one was done. Their gathering around was serving as a tent. I stood and laughed for a while and continued to the cinema. A new movie was about to show so I bought a ticket and went to sit. Strangely in all my sex escapades, porn movies weren't my thing. I was so much exhausted I only wanted a place to relax before going home. I saw an empty seat which I sat on. On the screen was a movie rolling. For a moment, I thought what on earth was going on. Everyone did their own thing and the movie did not have a point of focus. The room like in all cinema halls was pitch dark but for the brightness of the screen. I saw many guys being banged and others blow jobbing. Some sat down with locked lips and others were masturbating. It was like a football field with an array of activities going on.

I stood up to exit since porn wasn't my thing but on the door I met this guy who asked nicely why I was leaving so soon. He grabbed me and pulled me to the flat surface behind the cinema hall. I did not picture him so well and couldn't make him out on the spot. He hugged me and told me not to leave and in the process felt my dick and with excitement kissed me. We stood kissing and caressing for almost thirty minutes. Then he unzipped and sucked me and swallowed my sperms. Then he pulled down and made me to fuck him raw from the back. He held on to the wall as I thrust him from behind. Occasionally, he would push his ass up and down in a fucking motion to show approval of the penetration. I reached orgasm. We then sat on the floor for a while and later headed out. This guy was well-muscled and I knew he was a dark guy and had some locks too. We went out and to my amazement, in the light, here was Francis, my old Nigerian friend whom I had even met earlier the days. I couldn't believe it, but he told me he saw me and knew it was me. The state that I was in at that time, I couldn't even make his person out let alone his voice. He confessed to me he saw me enter and wondered if it was me actually so he also came in and just as I was leaving, he identified me by my dress and stature. We went on to Bond's Street to take a bus home. We were both shocked at each other. Both of us had hidden our sexual activities from each other for a long time. We sat chatting as he told me about some of the guys who were into same sex from the Rec. I was surprised but hey, life goes on. That night, Francis went home with me. We now were very open and took our shower together. We were so fond of each other so we had sex again in my shower. He told me how he liked me but couldn't say it because he wasn't so sure of my sexual orientation. He told me of the time he had peeped when I was accommodating him in my flat in the early days. He told me how he fantasized about my body each time I came out naked. He also told me how he fought the forces of attraction when we lay in bed together, but nothing happened in those days. I laughed it all off. That night, we were locked in arms and hugged in bed till we slept. Luckily, he had his off day and I also didn't work either. It was a heavenly coincidence just in time for us to restore stolen years of hiding.

Overtime, as we now found ourselves, he would sleep over sometimes and we would have a good time. I think we loved each other so when the opportunity presented itself, it was marvellous.

Francis wanted us to enter into civil partnership, but I didn't like the idea. For me, I was only living a life of fun and it didn't mean anything so serious to that extent. So he remained with his white guy Andrew till date but each time I was in London, we found time to meet and visit old times. I like Francis as a brother but was rather unfortunate, I gave myself up and out to him in such area of sex.

It was Francis who in fact told me of a pub called Underground around Brixton area. We visited it a few times. The most interesting thing about the place was that everyone entered either naked or in boxer pants. So at the entrance, one's belongings were put in a carrier bag and tagged for easy identification. It was a club and a gay one for that matter. I met many known faces I never knew were into same-sex affair.

There was this one time I got into a fun challenge in there where the winner and the loser would have sex in front of all the audience there. I lost the challenge and as destiny would have it, Francis' guy won so we had to fulfil the dictates. He was down and that helped so much so we got together which he was so much enthused about but I wasn't because of Francis, so Francis came close and told the audience the rules also allowed someone to relinquish his position and all that. I jumped on the clause and allowed him to take my place. They fucked on the bar and the rule also was that no pictures were allowed. It was like their sex sparked the animal in people. I could see people searching and grabbing others and a lot of things happening. All the same, I had a threesome with Francis and Andrew. The irony was that between him and Andrew, he was top but down when it came to me. Andrew was typically and always bottom; that is, at the receiving end or passive as it is termed. I was a typical top guy, always active as it is termed. Francis was the versatile one. He could adjust.

I once met my lady friend's brother at this club who wanted to have sex with me, but I ignored him. That would be so bad stooping low to that level, I thought. So even in some instances, one had to be circumspect who he got down with. But his sister never knew about his way of life and neither about mine. In this way of life, a lot of secrecy abounds and no one owns anyone up.

Most guys were tight-lipped guys except for those who go out to blackmail others for money or to disgrace. Blackmailing was actually a thing I saw in England; it was in Africa I got to know about it. It is so evil to do that per my opinion. I believe it is either you are gay or attracted to same sex or not. There was no need to fake or pretend to lure a genuine guy so you could rob him. In some instances in Africa, some victims got whipped, beaten and wounded. In extreme cases, they are killed by unknown assailants. That is the story of homosexuality in countries that it is illegal in Africa.

Repeatedly, I visited this place as it was the only time I could walk naked or partly so and not be bothered and each time it was with Francis. I later would enter free because I became friends with the manager of the place through sex. He had craved so much for my dick, I had no option than to offer him and also enjoy free entry to the pub. Nothing happened between us again, but I kept enjoying the free entry.

Soho also became a regular place of visit as there was so much to choose from. There were times I went to the Broadway shows and watched "Mary Poppins", "Mama Mia", "Sound of Music", "Les Miserable" and "Stomp" at different theatres. These are good shows and really entertaining. You may want to take a seat to watch in any theatre if passing through London.

## Paris

CJ visited and like he had suggested Red Light District, he also suggested we tour Paris. Since I love travelling, I embraced the idea. This time, we both didn't know where we were going but had to find a place of interest so we gave ourselves some time to google some places. Though I had worked there before and knew a few friends there, this time it was going to be fun trip and I didn't want to involve any serious business pals. After a few days, we agreed a weekend to visit Louvre Museum as our main centre of visit but not without some places of interest too so far as sex was concerned. I got to know the main gay stay place was Le Marais found in the third and fourth arrondissement. I also found the gay cruise club, Le Depot so we had those places too on our tour map. Then finally we had to book a hotel but luckily, Le Marais boasted of hotels and gay saunas which were also close to Le Depot, Les Halles the shopping mall and many other gay restaurants and bars. We decided to go by the Eurostar from London to Paris and this time avoiding flying. There was no limit to my sexual adventures and I would plan for all of them.

We arrived in Paris that faithful day and checked into our hotel, Hotel de Ville, close by Les Marais. CJ had come with another friend of his, Gary. We went for a suite with two queen-size beds so CJ shared his bed with Gary for the first night. After a short stay around the Banana Café and Place de la

Republique, and epicentre for nightlife catering for boys and men of all walks of life. It was a nice place and the only problem was the language barrier of which I was the best of the three. I had to display my little French here. We had arrived on Thursday and would be returning on Sunday. We decided to go to Le Louvre and it was amazing what the museum had to offer. It was huge and had endless collections just like the British Museum. I couldn't tell which had a lot of displays and still cannot till today. We enjoyed the trip because I had watched Dan Brown's "Da Vinci Code" and Le Louvre was well-captured and looked forward to seeing some of the stuff portrayed in the movie but did not see anything. Or maybe I didn't have much time to explore the whole museum as we had on our agenda to visit Le Depot, Bear's Den and if time permitted more other places.

We left Le Louvre after long hours of tour for Le Depot. The place was huge with live DJ; it had a large cruising area, some darkrooms, cubicles, dance floor, private cabins and glory holes. There was a lot to choose from and enjoy. But I was careful as there were strange people around. I call them strange because they sat alone or would look intensely and one could not know if they had come to enjoy themselves or probably there as spies or even to do evil. But we had to ignore them and went about our nightlife.

I preferred the dark room which the three of us stayed in most of the time. As dark as it was, I could see a lot was going on under the cover of darkness. We sat and conversed as the language was a barrier still until a white guy who spoke English fluently came around and joined us. He was our help that night as my poor French had been depleted and completed exhausted. He helped us with our buys and explained a lot to us. He informed us to be careful as there were pickpockets around.

This was so unusual of the many places I had been to. We had few drinks, danced to the French hip hop and came outside only for CJ and the white guy to go back. I stood with Gary till he went in to check on CJ. He came out laughing that CJ and the white guy were in the darkroom doing what we all expected anyway. Soon, they came out and we headed off to our hotel. The white guy who by this time was all into CJ came along and on our way engaged us in a conversation. It was nice to have him. So finally, he pulled up to our hotel room with us. He sat in the hotel's foyer for a while and headed inside. I did not bathe and went straight to bed. CJ then told Gary to join me as he shared his bed with Pierre.

Later that night, they were all up kissing and fucking. I tucked myself into bed but in the process I leaned over to Gary who I think interpreted it to mean that I was asking for sex so he welcomed it and we also got into action. We had the duvet over us and CJ couldn't see what was going on but could only imagine. There was no way he could also come over because of Pierre.

Gary was a breaker and mesmerised me. I have had many people blowjob me but he did what's called rimming. He played with the tip of my dick and as and when he felt I was about to ejaculate, he would stop and start to suck my nipple. He went on for a long time. This was some kind of love play. He was the sex type but I loved his approach as well. He would occasionally bite my nipple lightly, though painful but tantalising. Then he went down and enjoyed my meaty dick. In this round, I couldn't hold it anymore and spilled out all that I had been hoarding. He smeared it on me and held me close and we slept with it. It was a bit nasty to me as I had always cleaned up whenever I ejaculated, but it was also a new thing.

In the morning, it was all dried up on us and in the shower washing it off came with another hell of love making as CJ and

Pierre still slept. We joined them later, but soon our breakfast arrived so we ordered an additional mouth. We all had breakfast naked, I couldn't believe it. When we got up after the breakfast, I realised we all were hard stiff and it called for a group sex. This time, I wanted to fuck Pierre which CJ even initiated. We all took turns on him and he came across well-prepared and strong. Pierre begged to fuck one of us so Gary being so much interested in him offered his ass to be trounced by him. Pierre was versatile. We thought it was going to be a short action but we felt sorry for Gary as Pierre's never-stopping sex rampage on him took more than forty minutes. Gary could be seen biting the mattress in pain and Pierre would not stop. He was full of strength. It was like he punished Gary for all that we did to him. He ejaculated to the relief of Gary, but by then I was playing with his balls and started kissing him after he pulled out of Gary. Like I was on a mission to avenge Gary, CJ helped me as he held Pierre by the hands and I got into action and could see him sweating in the air-condition and blushing. I held my release several times to prolong the fuck. All this while, Gary lay exhausted. I then pulled out and played a bit and continued. This was going to last more than the time he had with Gary so most of the morning we were indoors. I realised he had some tear and this time felt great pains so I ejaculated and left him on the bed.

This time, like always with CJ, he wanted me to fuck him also. So I quickly gathered strength and gave some action to him as well but briefly. So we all went to shower down again afterwards. It was in the showers that Pierre complained I was a bit brutal as he felt too much pain that it changed his walking. We all decided to be indoors till afternoon. So we would have Saturday night out and by tomorrow would be returning to London.

That evening, Pierre took us to the Eiffel Tower area where

we had a nice night. The three of us returned to our hotel later only to prepare for our return tomorrow. Paris had a lot to offer in terms of cuisine, wine, nightlife, friendship and sex, but we couldn't experience them all. It needed to be enjoyed one after the other. I had been to Paris on weekends for the fun of it. It is a place sex is understood and people to me seem romantic and love sex.

We loitered around Le Marais, the gay district of Paris, for a while till it was late in the morning that Sunday. We took a taxi to our station and left early afternoon on the Sunday for London. It was all in all a nice trip and adventure to have embarked on. But London had always been home. It will always be my hood. I can move even with my eyes closed.

**New York**

New York was one of places I had always wanted to visit but not to stay. The Big Apple, as it is called, I planned to visit so I could have a fair bite off the big apple. That is the irony of it. The opportunity to travel came on the heels of a pastor who had ministered in my church I attended in London. I had sung during the service and he wanted me to minister in New York, in his church. With all the churchy stuff boiling in me, I relegated my sexual escapades to the background to concentrate on my mission unto the Creator.

I believe humans have a Maker to answer to and when the time beckons, no one tells you what to do and to do it right spiritually. There is a divine hand somewhere that controls the wings of time and the structures in tune. That was my belief. No matter what happens as a human being, there comes a time you yearn for a supreme being to intervene in some cases and matters. This tells me, there is a human yearn to fill a vacuum within creation to its creator. Whatever your belief or religion may be, this holds true in all its entirety and cannot be watered down because of different religious inclinations. We will be lying to ourselves in the process.

I had the shock of my life upon my arrival. I was met at the JFK Airport by a guy the pastor had sent. We boarded this traditional New York yellow cabs home. Meal was all set and was warmly welcomed. The night of the Saturday, I stayed in my room rehearsing some lines for the next day as I was to minister. The church was nice and welcoming. I rendered my songs one after the other to the applause of the congregation. I sang few known songs which they joined in. For a moment, I thought of my life as a minister of God, but that Sunday afternoon I changed my mind because of what transpired. But all through life, I have not had a calling into the Gospel ministry so tarried. I went for lunch outside with the pastor and few leaders since his wife was nursing a baby in Nigeria. The evening when we went home was the chronicles of this Nigerian pastor. I stayed in the house with him alone. I went to shower and as the toilet and the shower were in the same place but separated, he saw me shower as he entered to pass water. He shouted at me if he could join me. I was quiet as I thought he might have said it in passing. But that was not to be; even without any answer, he came to join me also naked. This was typical scene of reminiscence to me though. I couldn't believe because I had barely known him for a short time and moreover, this was a pastor who had preached in my church. So Pastor Uche Ikechechuku joined me. I knew it was a brotherly visit to New York and to do the work of God so I held an open mind to him joining me to shower. But that was not it. I had been mistaken as Uche tried touching my butt and then began sucking my nipples. In my wildest dream, I would have not believed it if anyone told me that, but here I was it was happening to me with no other person than Pastor Uche Ike as I called him. So this thing called same sex, I thought whether it was that a lot of people indulged in it and shied away from discussing and being found out or it is even religiously acceptable in some faiths. I shrugged that thinking off my mind because I know better that same sex is an abomination according to the Holy Bible. But things played out to amaze me and I thought a lot of people were into it but shied away because of public, society, church, family and friends' ridicule. We did what we would in the shower and stepped out. Uche then asked if I was surprised. I told him I wasn't in the least. He giggled to his room as I went to my guest room. I sat on the bed for a while contemplating whether I was dreaming or it was for real. Uche then called for me in his room so I went and stood by the door. He was still naked and told me to get over it. I laughed in my head as he approached me only to go down to do what everyone has been doing. I was surprised he knew all this. He sucked me well and then brought out some lube and condom and handed them to me. This time he wanted us to have sex so he applied the lube and rolled the condom over my dick which meant he was passive. So I did what I had to do begrudgingly because I was not happy I was doing this with a pastor but he was in the groove and enjoyed it. I will not forget this.

    I also wondered how he knew I would fall for his plots. A lot happened in his room to the kitchen and it was all fun. But I knew this pastor had a problem, a besetting sin he needed to get delivered from. The Bible clearly underlines God's hatred for homosexualism. It is termed sodomy in the Bible. I kept asking if this pastor had ever read it or not, but hey life goes on. Who am I to judge anyone? I wasn't God and I am not God but I know sin when I commit or see one.

Uche gave me a few bucks for my stay. He wanted me to spend a longer time. Knowing the calibre of his person, he couldn't go where I wanted to go. He was a pastor and I wasn't. I told him I wanted to sight see New York and even drove me to some places since he was free at daytime. I visited a few places with Uche. New York was too big to explore in a short time so I decided to only know some places. Obviously, Uche had gone with me to Central Park where we enjoyed some art, shopping and relaxation. It was such a huge place with numerous activities. We visited Statue of Liberty and Empire State Building. These were places Uche in his disguise and lies could and would go.

Later in the day, I went to Hell's Kitchen. The name fascinated me. It really was hell's kitchen. It was in Manhattan neighbourhood and I heard others call it Clinton and Midtown West as well but the name that resonates is the Hell's Kitchen which I learned a lot about. I realised the buildings in this area were six-storey maximum; this was strange. There was a lot to know and learn, but I settled at Hell's Kitchen Park and it was a great experience. Later in the evening, I visited some places; notably Therapy, Hell's Kitchen hot spot. There were so many gays bars, restaurants and gyms and other places of interest to spend the night. I also visited Industry Bar and XL Nightclub, all of which were great. Great gay people crowded these places but this time I couldn't go home with any except for some fondling in the dark parts of the bar and nothing more. For New York, I decided not to do anything so conspicuous that it could be traced to Pastor Uche by those who he served in the community. It would be a disaster for him so I lay low and rather visited the places that were designated for all and sundry.

In all, New York was great. I had a great time, great outing and definitely would visit again to explore more. I would visit without Uche so I can be freer and lodge in a hotel to enjoy more. But the entire visit was fun. I really enjoyed Uche too.

**Family**

One thing that has eluded my family is that no one knows my sexual orientation as I was careful to select who visited me and who I allowed to stay over. I did this well, combining both sexes so nothing untoward could be realised. Most people that visited me were friends and nothing much happened. There were some that were around when I was alone and we fucked. I had met a few guys online and invited them over. My parents had wondered why I had too many friends, but never questioned me since I was mature and in their eyes a good man. My siblings never questioned either. It was my younger sister who once jokingly said something but I brushed her off and till date there has been nothing more from her.

Talking about family, I had had sex with my younger sister when we were young. It was my sister who invited me to the bathroom and asked me to insert my penis into her. I must say, this was my first sexual encounter if I remember correctly. It is strange that some of the people I had indulged in sex and other stuff with pretend nothing happened or intelligently forget and are normal. To me, it is hypocrisy in the first order, because how in one's slightest imagination could one forget such an issue? We would hide to have sex as and when we wanted. This continued for some time, but we eventually stopped. We both didn't express such an interest as we grew so we stopped. But recently, my sister visited me and wanted to play with my penis, but I didn't allow her. She passed comments of me having a big dick and all that, hoping I would pull it out to disprove her but I didn't. I just wanted to avoid incest this time. The tendencies do come at times, but I have been able to overcome each time especially with my younger sister.

I have a younger sister and two brothers who I love so much. My love for them has caused me to be circumspect with my sexual orientation lest they find out and disown me. Well, I don't know what would happen if they should know but when the time comes, I will cross that bridge. For the moment, some things are better left unsaid. There are others that are better left unattended to till the time is ripe enough to pursue.

**University**

My university life was full of adventure from my first degree to masters. I am now undertaking a doctorate and these homosexual tendencies are rampant. I got involved with my professor one time and ever since, we have been having sex in his office. He gets me aroused each time he comes to class, but I wonder how he deals with his passions. I am still with him as he is unmarried.

I also got involved with my supervisor lady lecturer. She was married and whenever the husband travelled, she invited me. We always are home alone since her children are out for school. At times, I get confused as to what I really want whether men or women. I must confess I enjoy both.

I have slept with a few doctoral colleagues and I realise sex is just one thing people want all the time, but pretend all the time not to like it. It looks like it is a taboo to discuss or tag one with sex. It becomes very difficult even starting a sexual discourse; but when it is started, it never wants to end. So I ask, is it people are shy or per our nature and upbringing we shun it? If you should ask me, sex is good, nice, fun, rewarding, exhausting at times, private, and more importantly personal.

My school life has been good in terms of my grades so I could afford playing around sometimes. I had the luxury because I have always been thankful that God created me in a special way with a high intelligence quotient. I have always excelled and am grateful to the Almighty.

I cannot numerate the times I have had sex throughout my university life, but I can say 'a lot'. Sex life in university to me was the free range; no hiding, no recalls, no parental control, but it can also be a moment of waywardness and failure if care is not taken.

## Work

At my work place, from London to France, Ghana to South Africa and Botswana to Nigeria, I have had great sexual pleasure with my work colleagues who wanted it. It looks so much that somehow I meet like-minded people when it comes to sex. The work world adores this as in some cases for the ladies they tend to belong when they have relationships with their male counterparts. This is not to demean any lady, but this is what I gathered from some ladies I had an affair with. Some guys also find sex with their colleagues safer and protected. I have tried it all with men, women and people of different religions and nationalities. When it comes to sex, people tend to forget their religious beliefs and only remember when they have executed and sexually gratified themselves. I am also its part. Sex is a part of life and to me it is an integral part of life but not the most important part. I love sex to bits, but I am here because I seem tired and fed up with these entire sexual escapades, sir. All I want, sir, is to kill this sexual desire and animal nature that takes over me when it comes to sex. Is there a way?

This time, George Manfield was so emotional and sounded like a desperate person needing immediate solution. I sat to listen to him. I asked him if he really was done narrating his story. It was then that he interjected, saying there was more to say so I asked him to continue. I was telling myself it doesn't take another chunk of time but if even it did, it was my job as a counsellor to listen, deliberate and offer a possible solution. So George continued his narration.

He laughed and sighed. I wanted to know the whole story so I could offer help; after all, that is the reason why he sat in front of me.

**Friends**

I cannot say much about my friends because I see friendship as sacred and uttering anything means betrayal. If I should describe the times and persons, I know a friend would know about it. I want to reserve my experiences with my best friends but I can say for sure the story wasn't any different with friends in the church, work, and school and everywhere I found myself. It is amazing to know all these friends when I told them of my intention to write this book encouraged me, but pleaded I remove their parts from it or better still, pleaded anonymity. That informed me, they knew what they were doing was not right but for the fun and love, they succumbed. Though they bemoaned their dislike for all that had happened, they were also trying in their own ways to overcome their own demons. I remember one lady telling me that this whole sex thing "I think it is a necessary evil". She wanted to get out of this but loved it as well. Apparently, her sex life had given a lot to her in material terms and she was now torn in-between maintaining and receiving more or forgoing and depleting in resources.

People have issues they battle with only when they are alone. They feel so ashamed to share and fear condemnations as well. I have had sex with guys who will sit and pray with me after to ask for forgiveness. What does that tell you? They are sorry they did but wish to come out. Numerous church folks especially have done but they still find themselves in the act. I believe sex is a choice but when allowed to go out of hands between unqualified persons, the devil enters and magnifies it. That is what I believe. If that is not the case, why are so many people in sexual relations they are not happy about but still find it difficult to come out?

## Pornography and Escort

I never liked porn movies but I nearly ventured into acting in one. I saw the advert in London, responded, got the call and signed a contract and sent the whole contract back but never showed up. I thought I could make more money from acting. I ended up as an escort which also rewarded handsomely. With the escorts, I joined an escort group who would call me up each time they needed my service and I got paid later. My job was to accompany people to places and in the process, we went further into sex. That is, when the client requested. This was an escort company for both men and women, but the men's appointments were more. I met a few celebrities from all walks of life that I won't mention the names of for privacy's sake and to avoid any legal tussle. I met a few politicians. I met ordinary folks. In all, our oath or my oath was not to expose anyone so I cannot do so at this time. That is why all names used in this book have been changed to make it difficult to trace. But these were prominent people into soap operas, government and movie stars both from London and outside. Most of these dignitaries, who wanted escort, were from outside London though quite a number were also from London proper. There were a few clients who came from Hollywood, black and white from all walks of life.

It looked like people travel for fun from their cities and wanted unknown escorts. They wanted privacy and anonymity. Some of these clients came with bodyguards so that no escort could do or go contrary to agreed terms. I enjoyed the celebrity exposure and gatherings. Through this escort business, I had free tickets to many shows and film premieres. I became close pals with some of the clients for some time and still keep their numbers and emails. Occasionally, we communicate and as and when we find ourselves in close proximity, we meet up.

I loved escorting the footballers because it was great. Some afterwards by the nature of The Premiership couldn't openly come out as gays or as bisexuals so found solace in some escorts. I met with few of the footballers from the Premiership and the England Championships. I even took pictures with a few which I still keep. I don't intend to blackmail anyone like some do. It was work as usual and I respect their decisions and privacies.

I remember my first day at the escort orientation; one thing that the trainer hammered was secrecy, discreetness and privacy. Professionally, I have come to respect these and still abide by them. These footballers at times wanted some extreme sex which was daunting at times, but I had no option than to offer them. Some wanted to be fucked with strange instruments aside dildos. Some wanted some continuous unending sex which was demanding. Most of the footballers I met were passive guys and made my work easier. I met few African footballers playing in England at different competitions and levels.

There was this footballer I met who was also into music. He linked me up to some other guys and some musicians. I soon left dealing with the musicians because they most often were into drugs of all kinds. But all the same, I had my time with some.

Back in Ghana and South Africa, I also got involved with some stars into hiplife and gospel. It was funny some reggae musicians who spoke against homosexualism were themselves 'butty bwoys' as it is termed in Jamaica. The term 'butty boy' is an offensive word no man wants to be called. It simply means a gay person. I have had experience with musicians who even sang Christian songs but meddled in gayism. The list goes on.

**Fashion**

Another area that homosexualism and drugs exist is the fashion world. I ventured into a few modelling agencies. I got my profile made and had few contracts but didn't last there as my church elder advised against it. I was into high fashion and from the onset knew it wasn't for me. I wanted to keep myself and not be too much exposed publicly. But I can confirm that most fashion designers and creative heads in some of the fashion lines are homosexuals. Again, I cannot mention names and fashion lines. These are very powerful individuals with cash to spend when it comes to legal litigation. They will bury me so I rest it now. During fashion shoots and make ups, there was the probability that one would click with someone which would lead to sex or some relationship of a kind. I had been there and next time a brother, sister or friend wanted to get into fashion, I advised them well. I am not saying it is bad, but they should be well-advised and oriented to know their niche and what is good for them before venturing.

I love fashion. It is good. But it can be bad too. The

temptations in that industry are so great and vast. But still there are few who are innocent. I still would want to go into it again, but this time as I have learned a lot, I will make proper decisions.

## Fornication and Adultery

Fornication to me was normal. Adultery presented itself. I was surprised how married women still wanted sex outside their marriage and I have satisfied uncountable number of them who lavished me with all kinds of goodies. They gave a lot of cash, filled my fridge, took me shopping among others. Most often when I asked these married women why they wanted sex with me, the answer had always been wanting variety and to avoid the missionary sex position styles they were used to. These married women wanted the crucifixion, the doggy style and the professor. I am not here to teach these styles, but it sent a message to me that they were fed up in a way or other with their sex lives. Some confided in me of their sex lives being boring and one-way. For me, I had nothing to lose so I explored all the styles with them and this made me a hot choice. There are many married women on my list I see from time to time when their husbands travel. With some, I am even free with their husbands and are still good friends. These women pretend nothing exists when I am around and their husbands are least suspicious too.

I recently got to know that anyone who gets involve with a married man is a fool. The person has no head as the Bible puts it. These insights now guide me and have reduced my sex life with married women and soon I will cut all ties. It is a gradual process and no easy feat parting. After all, Rome wasn't built in a day? This is not to pat myself on the back to stay, but it needs a lot to cut ties. It takes time.

I feel so bad too because there was this one woman who got pregnant, but the husband refused to accept it and divorced her. It later came out that the husband had done vasectomy while in Belgium so knew instantly the wife was sleeping around. This woman couldn't say to anyone it was me and I dared not go forward because the husband is a business client even till today. I try to chip in a word sometimes for him to reconsider his decision with the wife, but he just cannot bring himself to think another man has been fucking his wife. I am sure he will kill me if he gets to know and learn this man always does business with him. This man is me. Because of this ordeal I am going through, the pain of wrecking someone's marriage and potentially causing death, I have decided to stop.

In stopping, I feasted on young women who were money-conscious. These were women from church and work places. There were others I met on the road occasionally and go to bed with. For this fornication, I am also stopping because I discovered again from the Bible that it is one such act that defiles the body; and he who defiles the body which is the temple of God will be destroyed, because God lives in this temple and as such cannot be used for such filthiness.

From the Biblical perspective it is bad but humanly, it is rewarding and enjoying. I have committed fornication to such threshold, the ladies were at my beck and call. Some I had sex with for free, with no contract or bond or gifts. Some I engaged not because of money they wanted but for the fun of it. These young women come along with fantastic sex positions that it will marvel the imagination. I wondered where they learned all these from. But these ladies were good in sex and in bed. They knew their stuff and will mesmerise you with their movements, strength and stamina. I have tried all such styles and positions. Some are even killer positions that they must be done cautiously.

I don't regret all these experience because I have learned a lot and now I can advise when necessary. There were times some of these women I fornicated with wanted me fucking them raw; in other words, no condoms and all that. Few I know got pregnant and told me but we had to abort them. Some ladies who tried to keep them strangely lost the babies in the process. At least three of such cases I remember. I always count myself lucky because I couldn't imagine fathering all these children with different women. I had no hand in these cases, the babies just didn't survive. I count myself blessed in so many things in life. I have been favoured by an almighty hand who rules in the affairs of men.

There have been some young pretty ladies who because of sex with me were not married. Some are still single but here I am, happily married. The irony was that they thought by their virtue of having a sexual relation with me, I would marry them. I feel sorry for wasting their time and redirecting their focus. But I still stand by the fact that they were all above eighteen years and as such, it was consensual. It was their decision and I don't regret the least. We play, we have fun but in the end, people (men and women alike) must be wise enough to discern and decipher when it is time to move on. If that doesn't happen, one will feel used and would have wasted time, precious time, for nothing. This is why you are reading this book to advise yourself or a brother or a sister, a father or a mother, an aunt or uncle or cousins at large. Time is precious and time is money. Time wasted or lost is irrecoverable. So be wise in time usage for work, church, fun etc.

## Older Women

One funny experience I won't forget was getting into older women, 'sugar mummy' they call it. One happened while I was at the university during my first degree. I was only nineteen years old then and got into a nurse of thirty-three years. She was so much into me and supplied virtually everything I needed on campus. My roommates were happy because her gifts were enjoyed by us all. There were times she didn't meet me and left my groceries and cash with my roommates. My mates knew I was probably in the next room with my '*inte*', that is, my girlfriend on campus, but protected me because of what they stood to enjoy. This went on for many occasions and my sugar mummy got fed up and left me. It was a relief because I was completely not informed about the relationship. As a nurse, she insisted we always use condoms during sex and it was at her house. She was unmarried. The day she told me of leaving, I was happy within because the whole relationship wasn't planned and I had been into it for fun and to prove a point to my mates. It was funny the things we could bet on and how things turned out. We challenged everything and got ourselves into unwanted stuff and relationships. We had sex with girls we didn't want to just for the fun of it, but after my fling with the nurse, I learned a few things which helped me.

The second relationship with a sugar mummy also came along when I was twenty-two and in level four hundred or final year. This was a school administrator at the admissions department. She was thirty-eight years old. With her, we couldn't be so open and had to be discreet because of the environment and the people around. Each time we wanted to have sex, she would go rent a hotel room outside campus and we would be there the whole day. She brought along food and drinks packed in the booth of her car. After we were done, she would hire a taxi for me to school with the groceries and cash as well. She was so protective and kept our relationship this way for the whole of my final year. Not even my mates knew about it. This administrator had two daughters and was so protective of them and discreet that she never allowed me into their house. But I knew the girls all right. They were at times even sent to me by their mum but nothing suspicious realised. This administrator I recall managed getting exams questions for me so that I would pass and pass well. Frankly, I did not need that and being against cheating, I never gave it out to anyone for fear of leakage and being caught. I did not have problems with my academics so it was very fine with me. Some of the questions I never glanced through. I didn't tell her what I did with the questions either. But in all, she was helpful and made my stay on campus great because I lacked nothing in terms of food, money and sex.

My last sugar mummy I had was a British who wanted us to get married. By this time, I was twenty-six years old and she was forty. She never was shy, but I was. This made it difficult to relate. We had fun, visited museums, Broadway shows and did plenty of things together. The love wasn't so much there unto marriage. Again I was a bit worried about our age difference and what my family would say, but she was very helpful during my early stay in London. We never had a problem but we separated and still meet up when we have free time on our hand. Jacky as she is called really was of a great persona. She had divorced and had a child. She was mature and knew what she wanted, but I was immature and was only playing along her terms. This was the last sugar mummy story and I don't intend on having any again. In my late thirties now, I wonder what the age of the next sugar mummy would be. I can see she would be quite old and cannot bear it comparatively to my age so I took the bow.

## Pornography and Dildos

I never liked porn in any nature; magazines, films and others. I preferred real action, but I found myself into pornography when I decided to quit most of my sexual escapades. I tried to shift away from real action with the thinking that I would finally come out of this habit of sex. I got into porn movies and my case worsened because each time I watched a movie, I tried testing out the position and all that it entailed. This time, I would watch porn with my partners be it gays or ladies. We would watch and act out what we saw. It was funny because there was always something new to try out. The positions, the screams and the forms of sex were not new to me but new because this time I sat to watch with a partner and acted it as well. One thing that stood out this time was the use of dildos. I would go shopping for different types, in different colour and sizes. I shopped for vibrators as well. I went for any new porn movie I saw on the market. I would watch post-paid porn movies from digital channels and paid with credit cards. I spent quite a huge amount in collecting my sexual movies and apparatuses. These I watched, studied and tried out at the least opportunity. My sexual life now moved into a different direction because these were all new to me.

I enjoyed every moment when I would insert huge dildos into my partners, male and female, with the screams and pains and it was all fun. They enjoyed them as well. I use vibrators on my ladies who giggle and scream for more. This was a new dawn for my sexual escapades. I am addicted to porn so much that whenever I watched without a partner, I would have to masturbate. There were times I never felt for sex but just watching porn turned me on. I used porn as refuge to avoid physical contact with people. This time I would masturbate instead. This continued and still continues. I have a wide collection of porn movies on CDs, mobile downloads and assorted porn magazines. There were times I watched porn with more than one person, gays and non-gays, and eventually had group sex afterwards. These movies would arouse many and many fell prey to porn then orgies followed. The porn industry was a huge money-making one and there are many great tycoons and investors with monies stashed in there. I don't know how this industry can be erased because for me it did more harm than good. I purchased porn about homosexualism, porn movies that some people had sex with animals, porn from all over the world; some were nice and others nasty in content.

**Past**

My past life had been nothing other than lies, sex, impersonation, work and academics. I combined homosexualism with bisexualism; heterosexualism with masturbation; fornication with adultery; good academic excellence with work laurels; incest with pornography; experimenting with anything that is sexually gratifying and sensually appealing; church with unseriousness and many more. I have tried sugar mummies and escorting; tried fashion and all that it comes with but never to come to a full realisation of myself until this present.

**Present**

"My life presently is a mess and seriously needs help, that is why I came to you," George reiterated. He sounded very down and just wanted some way of escape from his sexual escapades, but I continually reminded him it never works like that. It is a process with much devotion needed. George told me he presently is married but occasionally has gay sex, watches porn and gets involved with other women. He expressed sadness of wanting to come out this time. That was his present state.

**Beyond**

Looking into the future, he told me he would love to get rid of all relationships but the one with his married wife he was sure to maintain. He looked to avoid porn and stay away from many other activities which he narrated. I listened with rapt attention as I formed my remedies for him. He was looking into the future as a clean, happily married man with no baggage attached to him or weighing him down. It was encouraging because he was going all out to cut off these sexual escapades. These are habits developed over a period of time which need to be worked on one step at a time and over a period of time. I embraced the challenge and assured him of possibility and positivity.

**Religious Comparisons**

Now after George finished his narration, I tried drawing religious comparisons using the Qur'an and the Bible and any dimension reviewed put his actions in bad taste. It is not in my domain to judge, but everything George has ever done is never acceptable in any religious context but one great thing is that he has learned through the experiences and that has made him a great counsellor.

## Counsellor's Advice

The ideas expressed under this counselling session are some ideas of the author and not binding whatsoever but are trusted and tried remedies though.

Now my advice as he requested is that God never condemns anyone. Your admission of guilt and wrongdoing alone is a big step towards redemption. The problem is thus half solved.

For your sexual escapades, I cannot say much because as young and energetic as you were, you would have been better off if your energies were channelled towards a more profitable venture. It's never too late and not over until it is over paraphrasing Ashimolowo of KICC, London.

These energies if were well-harnessed could have been the x-factor in the equation of change and to change, but all the same there is always another opening. I see him as very lucky because he was under forty at the time he came to see me. At least if life really begins at forty, then his life was now beginning and there would be the need to enter the new life void of all the weightier baggage and luggage of unprofitability. George will need to know there are weightier matters to attend to at each forty than the frivolous chuff he has hung onto for a while.

Now back to various things raised, I can say with no fear of intimidation that homosexualism is not an inherent trait, but it is learned. Most youth are into this for the fun and think it is in vogue and trending. It is a sordid thinking so expressed through actions unwarranted. I am yet to see any guy who can claim he was born a homosexual. Others especially from Africa and Asia are into it for money because of the poverty levels.

I will disagree because that will defy divine order because if God wanted us to be gays, he would have created another man in addition to Adam than creating our curvaceous ladies to behold. No matter how one justifies homosexualism, there is no basis in the Bible or Qur'an.

Lies have been the basis for most of these habits. If the truth was expressed from the onset, then help would have been near. No need to start life with lies.

Incest, fornication and adultery are all mentioned and abhorred sins in the Bible.

The monies so spent on these sexual escapades could have been channelled into some investment by now to leverage a lot of things in George's life. Money is difficult to come by and must be used judiciously and with great care after careful planning and budget.

## Some Remedies

There is no one sure way of helping you come out of homosexualism or sexual immoralities. There are mentoring clubs with mentors and religious life coaches who can help but only when you will be open and forthright with. They will monitor and evaluate your progress based on what you furnish them with. There will be no privacy or secrecy again if you want to come out. Take the bull by the horn and face your demons and kill them. This time with another hand and mind to help you navigate through. What you navigate through boldly gravitates to success. Two heads are better than one.

When it comes to fighting addictions, behaviours and habits not needed, you cannot do it all by yourself and need an upper help, someone to encourage you, one to guide or direct and one to stand by and with you through it all. You will need help so that you don't overlook salient steps or actions to take. Normally, when one approaches me for a counsel, I consider few things like,

- Having to talk at length to understand issues by listening, first draw inferences and ask questions after.
- Tailor-make suggestions to suit situations and individuality. There is no one solution for all problems and there is the need to see through and satisfy individual needs based on likes, inclinations, beliefs, dislikes, willingness and maturity.
- Consider the knowledge bank of the person. I need to weigh your in-depth information and understanding to issues before prescribing any knowledge-based solution.
- Willingness of the person to give up. That is willingness to give up the homosexual or sexually immoral behaviour. If the person is unwilling, there will be no need to even begin any counselling session. Because no counsellor will want to start something he or she cannot finish or help stop or kill outright when it is bad.
- The seriousness and how open the person is, avoiding secrecy. The seriousness of the person to give up all acquired sexual materials honestly and without fail to destroy all by him/herself under close supervision. This helps to break the jinx of being tied to those materials physically.
- Will also have to ascertain how authentic the person's

story is. I believe any serious person will be serious about his story as no one stands to gain anything. In George's case, a few emails, pictures, phone calls, letters, some social platforms he joined were verified.

☐ Change is a process and time is needed. There is no way of rushing through a change process. If it is not well-built and established, there is the possibility of the whole process crumbling. Change needs strong foundation. The person must be willing to unlearn previous experiences and knowledge to learn new ones. Once they unlearn, the vacuum must be filled with profitable ideas hence a danger of a worse situation looms ahead. In any case, change is inevitable. We all must go through change, be it positive or negative. This time, it is the positive.

Below are some tested remedies, though not exhaustive and quite general:

1. Sincerely talk to a counsellor (religious counsellor). You may ask why I am specific about the type of counsellor. It is because psychologists and educationists try to agree with reasoning and understanding and try to please people. The truth is you are first a human before any tendencies. The human aspect of you needs a controlling force which can only be obtained from the Creator. After all, when you buy a machine and you cannot operate it, there is the need to consult the manual by the manufacturer. In the same vein, the creation needs consultation from the creator. When we talk about creation, we stress a supreme power brought down to us through religion; hence, a religious counsellor will help you to reinstate or identify yourself in the light of how the Creator created the creature. Because he created with no flaws. All the Creator did was perfect until the evil one contaminated it. This

is not to say social, psychological, academic, emotional, physical and other forms of counselling are not good. It is very much needed and important. I believe a religious counsellor who lacks in these areas mentioned will definitely complete it with the help from other experts. This helps to achieve a holistic approach to solve issues with counselling.

2. Sincerely, no one is born gay so if you have those tendencies and really need opting out, seek psychological and spiritual help. Show me a guy who claims he was born gay and I will discover when he started being one.

3. The first step is to ask for forgiveness. You may ask how? {Az-Zumar 39:53} from the Qur'an or seek the face of God and His forgiveness as the Bible admonishes.

4. Be honest and truthful and don't adore homosexualism or sexual immorality. Don't pride yourself with your accomplishments.

5. We need to be open with ourselves and avoid secrecy about our sexuality. Homosexuality is not an alternate lifestyle. It is wicked, evil and sinful and comes with pains and regrets. Go 'round and ask those who get fucked.

They feel so demoted and inferior. Some get all sorts of sicknesses in the life which lasts their entire lifetime. Those who fuck also are not without problems of sexual dysfunctions in later life and when needed most to perform, they slack. Above all, sexually transmitted diseases are on the ascendency. Most times when people approach me to counsel, I recommend a medical test first so as to know one's medical status. For George, he came clean in all tests recommended. He has been lucky and may not be lucky twice. You may not be as lucky as George so don't try it.

6. It is best to surround yourself with positive and straight-

thinking people. In other words, disassociate yourself from anything gay and gay tendencies, people, porn of all types and gay and sex websites. No one can force you, but it calls for deliberate steps. If it even means moving to another city or country, my dear, do it. Life is more precious and important than pleasures. Remember, a charge to keep (life) and God (Creator) to glorify. This must be your preoccupation in life.

7. Know that behaviour is a choice so is sexual, immoral acts and homosexuality. Choose wisely. If there is a need to change a behaviour, set personal boundaries to protect yourself. Have a counsellor, mentor, coach or a trusted friend to monitor and help you.

8. There is the need to also work on self-identity that is all embracing, pure and succinct. Man is but the friends he has. Man is but the books and counsel he reads and takes respectively. Man is but the food and places he enjoys. Know yourself, your identity, or let a counsellor help you discover yourself or better still rediscover yourself. Self-identity, self-image, persona, character, self-orientation, way of life are but all you need to be confident and positively focus.

**Moments of Truth: Tell-Tale Signs**

A great deal of problems exist that many people are silent about. All that glitters is not gold. What about considering these thought-provoking instances:

1. Many married men are gays or enjoy same sex
2. Many women are lesbians and cover up with titles like my 'girlfriend', 'sweetie', 'chocolate', 'darling' etc.
3. Many men who prefer anal sex with their wives need to be investigated. It is not for pleasure only but there is a

probability that they are bisexual or used to be homosexual.

4. Many men marry to cover up their homosexual behaviour. So not everyone married is insulated from the same sex. A lady friend had this to say, "All the handsome men are either married or homosexual." It may be slightly true, but it also may be partially flawed in thought and content.

5. Many married women entertain lesbianism with former partners whenever the occasion presents itself. Next time your wife or girlfriend keeps talking about a girlfriend all the time, take the time to investigate.

6. Many gay guys portray masculinity as a disguise to deceive. There is a general view that masculine and strong men cannot be gays, but my escapades have taught me they are even the bottom guys who play the feminine parts.

7. Many people who are advocates with passion either might have been a victim themselves, a son or daughter being a victim or might have been deceived by a gay. Inquire and learn more.

8. There are counsellors who also want to get into the minds of gays and will go to any length to siphon information from a homosexual. At times, their tactics may be unconventional because take it from me, most gays are secretive and unwilling to share their experiences, especially the very fine details George has shared with me. George's information given is in no way to look down on any gay but to tell the story mostly ignored. Just being candid can also set one free.

9. Many gays are very neat and well-presented. That is not to say some are not dirty.

10. Many gays have weird stuff as I call it scattered in their homes or work which other gays can easily detect so they click. Ask a counsellor to help you identify some. But from the top of

my head as I have known people over time, most gays have scented candles, teddy bears, funny under wears, weird key holders, and fanciful rings worn at specific fingers. Next time you don't know where to wear your fashion ring, ask a counsellor. This is but few mentions.

11. Gone are the days that gays wore very flashy and colourful dresses like peacocks, times have changed and the dressing of many can be deceptive. But believe you me, any gay can make another gay out by virtue of their actions or how they present themselves.

12. Don't be deceived that feminine-acting male guys are gays. They are not always so or true gays.

13. Watch out for coded chats.

14. Look out for short words and acronyms like LTR, G, WGT, BV, WV, Top, Bottom, Vers, Cock, Dick etc. the gay community understand. Understandably, these short words and acronyms have found their way into mainstream and unknowingly accepted by all. But those who are in the know, know them.

15. There are transvestite who are not gays and vice versa. Some only hide behind the veil to live their lives.

16. Look out for the type of magazines and movies people watch. Even when they fancy porn, find out what type of porn.

17. Know that homosexualism is not inborn but learned, so no one is insulated.

18. Look out for young guys who come across rich and tend to move with a higher hierarchy of men almost always. Not all are business meetings or counselling sessions, some end up in many diabolic ways. I know it may sound controversial, but I still stand by my idea.

19. People who love talking about sex are most likely to be

victims of sexual escapades. They look for channels to express themselves and once that chance is realized, they are never-ending talkative. Most of the time, the content and passion with which they express themselves matter.

# Conclusion

I really don't know why I wanted counselling but I needed to put down my feelings and intents into a book to help people identify with me and me with them. It was to help me express myself and be very open and, for that matter, to see reality as it has been. I hope no one will be offended by my graphic depictions and description and some stance. We all need help at one stage in our lives in various facets of endeavours. Mine was to get help and rid myself of sexual immorality and homosexuality. I don't know yours but whatever it may be, there is always help for you. Talk to me via my phone number or email address. The truth is, if I am unable to help you, I will surely direct you to another expert to help you. Thank you.

Just know that all my sexual escapades were not with juju or voodoo or other powers. It was my normal thinking that made me capable of doing all that. So if they think I possessed powers or consulted mediums, the answer is 'no'.

I am emphasising this because some use every means to do what they want but mine was without anything. My adventures took me far.

A *big* thank you to my counsellor; he has been of great help and I am highly indebted to him. He is a very plain, fearless and forthright person. The world needs such fellows. I will recommend him always to people struggling with various vices. He is so passionate and caring to go the extra step with you. He encouraged me to put this experience to paper and don't forget to check his advice incorporated in the whole script. They are invaluable, practically applicable, easy-to-follow ideas and knowledge and are timeless.

Thank you, Counsellor.